HEARTBEAT :

CONSTABLE ACROSS
THE MOORS

Nicholas Rhea

This edition first
published by Accent Press Ltd – 2008

ISBN 9781906373375
First Published in Hardback by
Robert Hale Ltd 1982

Printed and bound in the UK

Cover Design by Red Dot Design

About The Author

Nicholas Rhea is the pen-name of Peter N. Walker, formerly an inspector with the North Yorkshire Police and the creator of the *Constable* series of books from which the Yorkshire TV series *Heartbeat* has been derived.

Nicholas Rhea tells of some of the colourful incidents and eccentric Yorkshire characters encountered by a country constable, stories which provided the basis for the adventures of PC Nick Rowan, played by Nick Berry, in the TV series.

Peter N. Walker is also the author of *Portrait of the North York Moors* and, married with four children, lives in North Yorkshire.

Chapter 1

'O villainy! Ho! Let the door be lock'd; Treachery!
Seek it out.'
WILLIAM SHAKESPEARE (1564–1616) *Hamlet*

IN CRIME FICTION, THERE can be an element of drama and suspense when secret missions are undertaken by sterling heroes. For this reason, if for no other, I suppose it is the wish of every budding constable to become operationally involved with secrecy, spies, MI5, invisible ink and all the other trappings of undercover missions.

My first involvement was nothing like that. It began with the intolerable and incessant jangling of the telephone somewhere in the depths of an icy cold, dark and miserable office. That office lay at the foot of my staircase, and the start of my staircase lay pretty close to my bedroom door. My bedroom door, however, lay some five or six feet from my snug bed, across a large expanse of very cold linoleum. On top of all that, it was pitch dark and the hour was about five o'clock on a chilly winter morning.

These factors, plus the warmth of a loving wife beneath the cosy blankets, amalgamated to declare the telephone more than a nuisance. But shrilling police telephones cannot go unheeded, and as I lay in the darkness contemplating my next action, it became very evident that the person at the other end was another policeman. Other people, reasonable creatures that they are, would have stopped ringing ages ago; other people would have had infinite compassion for someone who'd been working late, whose family were infants and likely to be fully aroused at any minute, whose wife was cosy and warm and who personally wasn't too fond of climbing out of bed at five o'clock to answer silly questions.

But policemen aren't noted for compassion towards fellow officers, especially those of subordinate rank. When they ring other policemen, at whatever hour of the day or night, they keep the instrument active until somebody is compelled to do something about it. As I slowly realised my caller was a policeman, Mary also realised it was ringing.

'Telephone,' she burbled from a deep sleep. 'Telephone.'

'It's ringing,' I said, my voice talking to an empty black room.

'It might be urgent,' she managed to convey to me.

'It probably is,' I agreed, turning over. It was about this time that I realised it must be Sergeant Blaketon. No other person at Ashfordly Police Station would be so persistent. No other policeman in my section would ring like this; if someone's presence was required, they'd ring Control Room or get the night duty man to attend. No member of the public would ring like this, not for anything!

'Oh, for heaven's sake ...' Mary turned over. 'It's not the alarm clock, is it?'

'No, the telephone,' the house was full of strident ringing noises and I had horrid visions of Sergeant Blaketon hanging on to the other end, and equally horrid visions of him driving out to Aidensfield to knock on the door. That really would rouse the four children.

'All right, all right,' I snarled. 'I'm coming.'

Protesting, grumbling and angry, I slid my feet out of bed and my warm soles met the bitterly cold floor. The chill raced up my spine and did something to arouse me; I shivered violently. I couldn't find my slippers, and therefore elected to descend in my bare feet. I daren't switch on the bedroom light because Mary would hate me even more, so I made my erratic, bleary way from the room and down the stairs, unerringly guided to ground level by the nerve-shattering din.

I fumbled my way across the hall and found the light switch. My frosted feet made their way across the bitterly cold composition floor of the office and I stretched a hand towards the noisy contraption.

It stopped ringing. A weird silence sat among the darkness of my house as I blinked in the light of my office.

I had heard many legends about telephones ceasing to ring just as the recipient reached it, but in circumstances like this?

I stood and stared at it. I dared it to recommence. My feet had started to turn into blocks of ice, and the awful cold was producing goose-pimples in very strange places. Nothing happened. And so, as I waited for the next sequence in this domestic drama, I could look out of my office window. The light showed a vast area of white and I groaned. Snow had fallen. Beyond my four walls, several inches of moorland snow had arrived unannounced and graced my weed-ridden garden. If this was a call-out, I could justifiably say I was snowed in. I realised today was Candlemas Day, February 2, and my mind quoted the local weather prognostication – 'If Candlemas be fair and bright, winter shall have another flight. If Candlemas be dull with rain, winter will not come again'. I wondered what sort of summer we could expect when Candlemas was thick with snow.

I must have waited for five long minutes because my feet appeared to be growing detached from me, and the telephone sat very still. So, it hadn't been a policeman after all. It must have been somebody else, somebody who'd given up, somebody who'd dialled 999, or who'd changed their mind.

Smiling, I turned towards the beckoning stairs. I thought of my welcoming Mary in her cocoon of bedclothes; she was just lying there with an overwhelming desire to warm my feet with her lovely back. This made me hurry up stairs. Out went the office light as I galloped back to bed, thankful for the consideration shown by this unknown caller.

As I reached the bedroom door, it began again. The incessant ringing resumed with evident determination and this time I raced down stairs, angry and upset that the world was so full of inconsiderate, demanding people who should know better.

'Police!' I snarled into the mouthpiece.

'Rhea?' It was Sergeant Blaketon. He sounded very wide awake, and I wondered for an awful moment if I should have been on early patrol route, but a glance at my diary revealed the truth. I was shown as late turn, starting at two this afternoon.

'Yes, Sergeant.'

'Did I get you out of bed, Rhea?' he asked blandly.

'No,' I growled. 'I was taking the budgie for a walk.'

'There's no need for insubordination, Rhea, this is urgent.'

'Urgent, Sergeant?'

'Very urgent and very important. Get yourself down to this station for six o'clock, bike and all. Bring a packed lunch and some hot soup. It's an all-day job, and it might take us until night. Be equipped for snow.'

'Snow, Sergeant?'

'Snow, Rhea. There's five or six inches out here.'

'What sort of job is it, Sarge?' I dared to ask.

'I can't discuss it on the telephone,' he informed me. 'Just be here at six.'

He put down his phone and I looked at my office clock. It was ten past five. For a few moments, I stood on the cold floor and stared outside. I could see snowflakes descending in the patch of light cast from the office window, and their beautiful smooth movements mesmerised me. Then Mary was shouting at me from the top of the stairs.

'What is it, Nick? Is it my mother?'

'It's worse,' I called back. 'It was Sergeant Blaketon.'

'What's happened?' There was genuine concern in her voice.

'I've got to go out. It's something important and he won't tell me over the telephone. I've got to be at Ashfordly office at six, equipped for an expedition of some kind. I need soup and a packed meal, and snow shoes by the sound of it, or skis.'

'I'll pack something, you get ready.' She was a picture of composure as she switched on the stairs light and descended. How she managed to look so calm, I'll never know, although it might be linked with the fact that she'd had to discipline herself to wake at all hours

5

to night-feed four children over several years.

I trudged upstairs and entered the bathroom. The mirror was frosted over, so I breathed on it and my breath frosted over too. I shivered violently and decided against shaving. A miniature beard would keep me warm – I'd seen 'Scott of the Antarctic' and the frosted beards of his courageous crew. I might be like that.

By quarter to six, I was dressed for an Arctic expedition. I wore my pyjamas beneath my uniform, a device employed by generations of policemen who'd patrolled in sub-zero temperatures for twenty-five winters or more. On top of it all, I had dressed in my official motorcycling suit. This was a large black rubbery outfit which smelled of oil and made me look like a paunchy grizzly bear. It was a two-piece suit with seamless trousers and a long tunic which concealed almost everything. Gauntlets protected my hands, and I sported a large round crash helmet with POLICE across the front. This was to protect what few brains I had. On my feet, I selected leather boots with rubber over-shoes. Thus clad, I had great difficulty in walking normally, but felt no one would notice me at this early hour. I was ready for my mission of mystery.

'Where are you going?' Mary asked, hugging her dressing-gown around her slender body.

'I wish I knew.' I meant every word. In my arms, I carried my packed lunch and three vacuum flasks, two with soup and one with coffee. Apples and chocolate bars were stuffed into sundry pockets and I had managed to find a packet of dates in the pantry.

'I'll try to find a telephone.' I wondered if they had telephones where I was going.

'Bye,' and she tried to kiss me across the paraphernalia which cluttered my frame. I stooped

6

awkwardly and plonked a chilly kiss on her forehead.

'Bye,' and I opened the front door.

A huge drift had gathered against the door and nearly fell in as the stiff breeze whipped small whirls of floating flakes into the house. Outside, the garden was a white desert, endless and fascinating, but definitely not the sort of conditions to encourage the riding of motorcycles. But orders were orders and one's constabulary duty had to be done. I slammed the door before Mary was overcome with drifting snow and had to kick the drifts away from the garage doors.

After twenty minutes of hard labour, I succeeded in scraping away sufficient snow to permit the doors to open and I slid my meagre rations into one of the panniers of my bike. A line of drifting snow followed me into the garage, so I hurriedly straddled the machine and kicked it into life. It fired first time, a tribute to our police mechanics, and I guided the Francis Barnett from its cosy home. Together we braved the fierce black morning with its blanket of pure white, and it was a daunting experience.

The doors blew shut behind me and the resultant clatter must have told Mary I was on my way. The tiny machine phut-phutted into the deepening snow and I hoped I knew how to cope. There's an art in riding motorcycles in snow, and it is an art acquired painfully by many years of falling off or skidding into ditches. By use of gears, feet, body weight and accelerator, it is a marvellous experience to safely negotiate a well-tuned motorcycle through heavy drifts, up and down slippery slopes, past other vehicles and across wide expanses of virgin snow. But there was no guarantee I would achieve any of those aims.

Sometimes I stood on the footrests to allow the bucking, slithering machine to perform its gyrations beneath me, and at other times I lifted my feet off the rests and carried them slightly above the surface of the road, to keep me upright if the wheels decided to travel away from me. Surprisingly, my bike and I remained upright.

I moved steadily and enjoyably through the falling snow. The headlight picked out weird and grotesque shapes among the drifts, the heavily clad conifers, the smothered hedgerows and the undulations of the highway. But I was alone, so utterly alone among virgin snow, and knew care was vital. My exertions in maintaining both movement and balance made me perspire heavily beneath the heavy clothing, and by the time I reached Ashfordly Police Station, I was lovely and warm from my five-mile struggle against the best of winter snow. The fact that I was warm made the journey less onerous.

I parked my precious machine against the office wall and entered the welcoming brightness. A flickering fire glowed in the grate and the place reeked of warmth and cosiness. I stood in the entrance and Sergeant Blaketon bawled, 'Get out, Rhea! Look at you ...'

I looked. I was caked in white. In spite of the windscreen, my motorcycle suit was frozen solid with a thick layer of crusty snow and my unshaven face bore icicles in abundance. But already, the heat was making them melt, and they began to drip on his clean, polished floor.

I went outside and jumped up and down to try and shake off my winter coat and managed to dislodge some of it. Then I re-entered and in the porch, removed my suit, managing to drop lumps of snow all over the doormat.

'You're late,' said Sergeant Blaketon as I entered

8

anew.

'I had to dig my way out of the garage, Sergeant, and the road down here is full of drifts and is treacherous in places.'

'Then you should have set off earlier. I do not like shoddy timekeeping, Rhea. You should plan ahead.'

'Sorry, Sergeant,' I said, knowing better than to argue with him.

There was no one else in the office and I wondered if I was the only participant in this curious enterprise. I went behind the counter to look in my docket and there was no correspondence, but Sergeant Blaketon had vanished into his own sanctum.

'Come in here,' he bellowed, and I obeyed.

I stood smartly by the side of his desk and he handed me an envelope. It was a small buff one with my name neatly typed on the front and it had the word SECRET in red ink across the top. If this was a red-ink job, it must be important.

'Open it, Rhea.' He smiled fleetingly.

I did. Inside was a piece of paper with SECRET splashed in red across the top. It was addressed to me in person.

I read it most carefully, for I'd never read a secret document before. It told me to report to Sergeant Blaketon at Ashfordly Police Station at 6 a.m. today.

I looked at him, and he looked at me.

'It says I've got to report to you, Sergeant,' I said foolishly.

'Yes, well, here you are and you have reported.' He saw nothing odd about this initial encounter, for his rule-bound mind never looked for the odd or the strange. He obeyed orders and never questioned them.

'Right, Rhea,' he said. 'Remember this and don't

write it down.'

He coughed, cleared his throat and faced me squarely across his desk.

In these moments of history, I stood before him and tried to look interested. I hoped to God I would remember what he was about to impart.

He coughed again. 'This is secret,' he said, looking anxiously about himself. I wondered if any more snowmen were about to arrive. 'We have learned from reliable sources that the Russians are very anxious to infiltrate our Ballistic Missile Early Warning system. They have already made several attempts, and one of their reported techniques is for a Russian ship to signal our coastguards with a report that a man on board is ill. They say he suffers from appendicitis or something which requires urgent medical attention, and the man is brought ashore. Several of his colleagues accompany him and we have learned that they don't all return. There are no Customs and Excise Officers on the remote parts of this coast, Rhea, and detailed checks are impossible. We believe the Russians are coming ashore to do something to the Early Warning Station.'

He paused. I wondered if he'd been reading too many spy thrillers, although I had read of this attempted infiltration method in the newspapers.

'Last night, Rhea, at ten o'clock, such an incident happened. It was observed by the coastguards and they report that twelve men arrived with the sick sailor, but only eleven returned. One is still ashore.'

'So we've got to find him?' I realised my mission for today.

'Yes. We have mustered men from all over the county, and each man has been given specific instructions. Your duty is to proceed to the area of

Swairdale Forest. You must make a search and remain there until you are dismissed. Keep searching, checking, looking for footprints, meeting places, cars, anything that might suggest a link-up between the Russian immigrant and his contact. He might be meeting an accomplice, placing a letter in a collecting place, anything. You know what spies are.'

'And if I find him, Sergeant?'

'Arrest him, of course!'

'With my bike? Where do I put that? I can't sit him on the pillion ...'

'Radio in, duffer! What's the radio for? Radio for help and we'll send a car.'

'In this snow, Sergeant?'

'Look, Rhea, you are not paid to think. Just get out to Swairdale Forest and start looking.'

'What's he look like?' I dared to ask.

'We don't know. Just stop all suspicious characters and question them. If in doubt, raise Control. Oh, and prefix your calls for this mission with the code word 'Moorjock'.'

'Moorjock, Sergeant.'

'Good. You've got it?'

'Is anyone else in Swairdale Forest?'

'Just you, Rhea, and a few animals and birds.'

'No more men?'

'No, there's acres of pine trees. Your boundary is the forest itself and it includes the minor roads which join the main road from Strensford to Eltering. It's a big area, Rhea. It's just below the Early Warning Station which means that if he gets past our lads nearer the coast, he could confront you. A lot could depend upon your professionalism.'

I asked him all kinds of questions, but it seemed I

was on my own. I had a long period ahead of me, a period when I'd be climbing mountains, riding across moors, dodging bogs and marshes and winding my way between rows of Forestry Commission conifers. I knew the forest well. On a fine day, it was gorgeous, loaded with the scent of pines and replete with a multitude of wild animals and birds, ranging from deer to dormice and jays to jackdaws.

I had an Ordnance Survey map in my panniers, one I always carried, and after a quick cup of tea with Sergeant Blaketon, I climbed into my cold, stiff motorcycling outfit and trundled into the bitterness of this cold February morning.

Outside, I had the world to myself. The roads were covered with a smooth white layer of new-fallen snow and they stretched interminably ahead of me. Riding carefully and treating my expedition as a test of motorcycling skill, I covered the long miles at a reasonable pace. The heavily trod tyre on the rear wheel bit into the soft, virgin snow and the delicate surface presented no real hazard. The disturbed snow flew about me in a fine cloud, clinging to my suit and my face, and enveloping most of my machine in the purest of shrouds.

Surprisingly, I was not cold. Although the morning was bitter in the extreme, it was a dry cold, something on the lines I imagined in Antarctica or Alaska, and my unfailing efforts to retain my balance and to keep the Francis Barnett moving forward made me perspire deep inside my heavy layers of protective clothing. My face, however, was cold; the biting wind of a new dawn attacked my cheek bones and nose, and it battered my ears.

But I cared not, for I was enjoying myself. I gloried

in the experience of an uncluttered highway, for there was not a vehicle to be seen. I wondered at the silence beyond, the privacy of a new dawn in the moorlands of the North Riding, and I was flushed with pride at winning my contest with the slithering bike beneath me.

Soon after six thirty, I left the valley and climbed to the heights. Knowing how rapidly the winter snows obliterated the elevated landscape, I turned off the main road with some trepidation, and as the dry winds moved the light snow around in whirls and drifts, I found myself having to take fierce survival action. When I was confronted by a thick drift, I would kick my way deep into it while astride the bike, somehow holding it upright with the other foot. Then I would trundle the bike backwards, and accelerate many times towards the obstruction, literally bulldozing my way through.

Usually it worked. I would hurtle into a deep drift at a fair speed, and after repeated efforts, the bike often carried me to the other side. Through this kind of energetic progress, I reached the turn-off point for Swairdale Forest.

This was one of the extremities of the boundary in which I had to patrol to hunt the Russian during the coming twelve hours. I turned into the narrow, snow-filled lane and this took me deep into the forest. The road was bordered by tall pines and soft larches, interspersed with bare silver birches and some heavy broom shrubs. As I dropped from the exposed moorland road, there was less snow on the ground, much of it being caught in the evergreens above me. The trees were thick with suspended snow and as my motorcycle roused the sleeping birds, they moved off, startled by the noise but more startled when large dollops of snow fell on them.

They fell on me too; it was like being bombarded from above by dozens of children hiding aloft with arms full of well-aimed snowballs. Maybe the Russian was up there? Perhaps he was aiming snowballs at the defending forces? I'd get him if he was!

I glanced skywards with a smirk on my face and fell off my motorcycle.

Through not concentrating on my route, I was late into a twisting corner at a point where the road turned left and dropped suddenly and steeply. The whole episode was deeply embarrassing. I hoped the Russian wasn't watching.

The motorcycle, with its engine roaring, back wheel spinning and lights blazing, began its independent descent of that hill. I was nowhere near it. It slithered away, and was kept on the road by the high sides and the drifting snow. As I staggered to my feet, I watched my transport hurtling noisily down this one-in-three gradient and I began to follow. In my eagerness, I moved far too quickly. My feet left me; by some unaccountable feat of gymnastics, both my feet left the ground at the same moment and elevated themselves to waist level. Somehow, they stuck out in front of me and pointed at nothing in particular. Momentarily, therefore, I was suspended in mid-air surrounded by snowflakes, and then I abruptly descended. My well-cushioned rump connected with the slippery slope and the smooth rubbery nature of the motorcycle suit was totally incapable of gripping the ice beneath me.

I started to slither down the hill. I was in hot pursuit of my motorbike and wondered if I would gain on it, or even catch it! Its weight and roaring engine kept it sliding majestically onwards but I was moving at a fair pace too. I was kicking my legs in the air, waving my arms and trying my best to seize something which might act as a brake. But I was too far into the centre of the road. Nothing came to my aid, and there was no way I could halt this downward race. In fact, I think my automatic gesticulations served only to speed me forward.

The wind rushed about my face and ears, and I remember seeing hints of daylight through the thick trees. I remember noticing the flashes of its headlight as the plunging motorcycle followed its predetermined route and I realised there were better ways of spending my time before seven o'clock on a morning. Then there was a tremendous crash as my bike collided with a milk stand.

Three large milk churns were standing like sentinels on that stand. They were empty and awaiting collection this morning, but as my rampaging motorcycle assaulted the stand, two of the churns rolled off some yards ahead of me. They now began to roll down the hill. They rattled and bounced until their lids fell off and rolled in their wake. The din was awful. The clanging of the churns, the roar of the motorcycle engine and my shouting caused wild birds to race to safety from an unknown enemy, and their urgent flappings sent huge dollops of snow from the trees. It was snowing snowballs that morning.

I sailed past the milk stand in fine style. I must have been doing a good twenty miles an hour on my bottom, and I was reminded of my childhood sledging days, except I didn't have a sledge. I could not stop; I followed the erratic route of the milk churns and noticed one of the lids bounce into the woodland and vanish. The other continued to roll downhill, bouncing like a child's runaway hoop.

As I continued downhill, I realised the motorcycle had stopped and I could hear its engine behind me. It was now stationary in its garage beneath the milk stand, and eventually I halted. I terminated my journey quite sedately and quite smoothly in a dumpy holly bush which grew from the side of the road. As I closed my eyes to lessen the drama, I vanished into the depths of this prickly-leafed plant and found myself wrapped awkwardly about its sturdy trunk.

The milk churns continued for a further distance and rattled to an eventual halt somewhere out of sight. I ceased worrying about the churns and concentrated upon extricating myself from the embraces of the holly bush. It was not too difficult because I'd smashed a lot of branches on the way in but the road surface was treacherous. This was the root of my continuing problem. It was like glass; I guessed rain had fallen last night, or snow had melted on the road surface, and the night's frost had frozen it solid. The light covering of snow had done the rest, and tons of snow remained up there, to be knocked down by terrified birds. Dollops continued to tumble from the pines as I gathered myself together.

I could hear my motorcycle phut-phutting somewhere out of sight, and began to make my panting, breathless way back up the hill. I fell several times. My feet refused to grip the surface under any circumstances, and I spent several minutes propelling myself forwards with rapid movements of my feet, only to find I hadn't progressed at all. So I took to the trees.

My eyesight had become adjusted to the gloom of the forest, and by using healthy young conifers as banisters, I gradually hauled myself up the slope towards the bike. By now, it had stopped phut-phutting, but the lights still burned and guided me towards it.

My only problem was getting across the road. Gingerly, I left the security of my trees and stepped on to the steep, treacherous surface. And my feet whipped away once again. Down I went, hitting my backside on the ice and once more spun down the icy slope. This time, I was twisting and turning like a spinning-top as my arms and legs acted like flails and completely failed to halt me. I thought of milk churns, holly bushes, holes in the seat of my pants and Sergeant Blaketon's Russian as I hurtled once more to the foot of the slope. I concluded this second journey in the same holly bush in approximately the same state as before. I spent some time sitting in that bush pondering my next move.

I couldn't leave the bike because it contained my soup and flask, and it also bore the radio which was my lifeline. I could wait until dawn and the possibility of a snowplough and gritter, although I knew the ploughs arrived here about twelve noon. They had to clear miles of major roads and visit umpteen villages before bothering with such remote areas as this. I could spread gravel or salt upon the ice, but I had no shovel …

Besides, it was still dark and I could not see very well, although dawn was not far away. I made my decision. I would try again.

This time, I made my nervous crossing of the road at a point very close to the friendly holly bush, and found I could make progress if I walked on all fours. If one foot slipped, the other and my two hands coped with the situation, and so I gained the other side of the road. There, I copied my earlier climb. I clung to the trunks of small conifers as I hauled myself through the thickening snow towards my precious flasks of soup and coffee aboard the stricken motorbike.

I made it. In the grey light of the coming dawn, I could distinguish the outline of the rough wooden table which had borne the milk churns, and beneath it was my fallen machine. The headlight and tail light still burned brightly and spread a patch of warm orange and red on to the snow. The lights also showed that it was still snowing. I gingerly stepped on to the verge and by holding on to the side of the stand, found I could maintain an upright position. I was making good progress.

My next task was to haul the bike from its resting place. Luckily, the Francis Barnetts of that ilk were not too heavy and the ice beneath it enabled me to drag it clear of the stand. By pressing my body against the milk stand, I could lever myself into a position where I could seize the fallen machine and haul it to its wheels. I coped surprisingly well and propped it against the milk stand. So far, so good.

Next I examined it. With a torch taken from the panniers, I found the machine had fallen on to the side which contained the tools and spare clothing, and so my soup and coffee flasks were intact. There was a scrub mark down one of the leg shields, and the windscreen was broken about halfway up. I never found the missing bit.

But otherwise, the machine was in surprisingly good condition, and perfectly capable of being ridden. Dare I ride it down the hill? Or should I wait until the roadmen came with grit and salt?

But when hunting Russian spies, one does not wait for British workmen. So I decided, in the interests of the security of the nation, to guide my motorcycle to the bottom of this tricky slope.

It would be best to ride it, I decided, but I would sit

astride in a low gear with my feet on the road surface, and allow the gears to hold the machine at a low speed as I allowed it to find its own way to the bottom. Gravity would achieve a lot, I reckoned.

And so, having checked it thoroughly once more, I gingerly sat astride, by using the security of the milk stand, kicked it into life and moved off. I eased it most carefully on to the snow-covered ice which now served as a road, and smiled to myself. Everything was going fine, just fine.

Then it slipped. Without any warning, the front wheel slithered away and I clung to the handlebars as the bike fell over yet again. It dislodged me, but I wasn't going to be deterred so easily. I hung on.

I am not sure how I managed it but I found myself squatting on my haunches, with both feet firmly on the ground, hanging on to the handlebars of the bike which lay beside me. Its footrest, pannier and leg shield were bearing its weight and it was sliding smoothly down the hill, taking me with it. And so we moved like that.

The bike continued its descent through the trees with me steering from my squatting position almost beneath it. I partly supported its weight as I hung on for grim death, and we sailed down that slope in fine style, the bike's light picking out the trees, a milk churn lid halfway up a fir tree, the trail of one churn leading deep into the forest and the lofty trunks which supported a canopy of thick snow. But we made it.

My bike and I safely negotiated that steep hill in our outlandish style and we glided to a smooth standstill at the base, very little worse for our experience. I must have lost some material from the seat of my pants and from the soles of my boots, and the bike had shed half a windscreen and some slivers of paint. Some petrol had spilled out too, but the engine worked and the lights lit my route ahead. I was mobile.

I had no idea how I would climb back up that hill or up any other hill, but that was some time in the future. Right now, I could continue my journey deep into the forest, hunting the Russian and serving my nation with unstinted loyalty.

The Forest of Swairdale occupies a large tract of land in the bottom of that valley. Planted by the Forestry Commission, it comprises row upon row of immaculate pines, spruce and larch, all in symmetrical rows. Nothing else grows beneath them, and they cover the land with a deep blanket of dead pine needles, through which very little grows, other than a few fungi and blades of brave grass. As a moorland valley, it would be no good for agricultural produce, so its reclamation years ago from heather and bracken had been beneficial due to the timber it currently provided.

Indeed, a little village community flourished here. Due to the work brought to the valley by the Forestry Commission, a group of people live and work deep in the forest. They occupy cosy wooden homes which look like log cabins, and the community has a post office-cum-shop with an off-licence for liquor. Having arrived safely in Swairdale, I parked my machine near a gate and performed a walk-about patrol. It was half-past seven and the place was coming to life.

I spent an hour or more in the village, drinking coffee in a forestry worker's cosy home, finding the farmer to whom to apologise about his milk churns, and asking everyone to let me know if they noticed a Russian skulking in the woods. By eight o'clock, I had warned everyone, and returned to the motorcycle.

The radio was calling me.

I responded; it was Sergeant Blaketon.

'Location please, Rhea,' he asked, speaking through the courtesy of Control Room via a system known as Talk-Through.

'Swairdale,' I said.

'Down in the valley, you mean?'

'Down in the valley, Sergeant,' I confirmed with some pride.

'I never thought you'd make it in this weather,' was his remark.

'Neither did I, Sergeant.'

'Look, Rhea, you know the Moorcock Inn?'

'I do, Sergeant.'

It was not far from here as the crow flies, but in fierce moorland weather, it would be isolated and beyond the reach of anyone. It would be like riding to the North Pole.

'I want you to call there,' he said softly.

'I'll never get there, Sergeant, not in these conditions,' I protested.

'It's vital, Rhea, very important. You must make the effort, and that's an order.'

'Is the Russian there?' I put to him.

'No, but there's a bus load of businessmen lost up there. They went to Strensford last night for a conference at the Royal Hotel, and haven't returned home. We checked, and they've left the Royal Hotel, but they haven't got home to Bradford. We can't make contact with the Moorcock Inn because the telephone cables are down, due to the weight of snow. Seeing you're in the area, we thought you might pop in to see if they're there. Lives could be at risk if they're not located.'

'But it will take hours, Sergeant!' I tried to protest.

'Then get going immediately, Rhea. Look, you'd better do something – one of those missing men is the Chief Constable's brother.'

'I'm on my way,' I said.

At first, I thought there was no way to the Moorcock Inn other than by the hill down which I had travelled so dramatically with the milk churns and burning trousers, but I pulled the map from my pannier and examined it. My boundaries were clearly defined, and as I pored over the details, I discovered a forest track which led from Swairdale high on to the hills. It cut through the dense trees and then crossed the open moor at a point close to the summit, emerging at the top of a steep hill. The Moorcock Inn lay mid-way down that hill on the main road to Strensford.

I knew the forest route would be rough and for that reason it would provide traction for my wheels. Beneath the trees, there would be a minimum of snow. Having satisfied myself that the Russian was not lurking in Swairdale, I set forth upon my diversion to the isolated inn.

Surprisingly, the trek was possible. The heavy snow had failed to penetrate the ceiling provided by the conifers, and although a light covering did grace the route, it was negotiable without undue difficulty. I trekked high into the forest, standing on the footrests and using the machine in the manner of a trials rider. The action kept me warm and cosy, and after two miles of forest riding, I saw the summit ahead of me. A tall wire fence ran across the skyline and this marked the end of the woodland; beyond were untold square miles of open moor.

My forest track ran towards a gate in the fence and I halted there to open it. I checked again for the Russian –

there was not a mark in the snow; no spies had passed this way. In fact, no one had passed this way. I went to open the gate.

It was locked.

A stout iron chain was wrapped around the tree trunk which formed the gatepost, and the chain was secured with a gigantic padlock. There was no way through. And the fence stretched out of sight in both directions.

I was completely stuck. I could ride all the way back to Swairdale but would never negotiate that steep hill to regain the main road; besides, that route emerged miles from here. I hoisted the bike on to its stand and walked along this perimeter fence, but there were no breaks. It had been erected recently and was totally motorcycle proof. Then I had an idea.

I looked at the hinges of the gate. Two large hinges were secured with long screws, and they were fastened to the other post, the one which did not bear the chain. With no more ado, I found the screwdriver and began to remove the hinges. It was the work of moments. In no time, I had both hinges off and swung open the gate, its weight being borne by the massive chain at the other end. I wheeled my trusty machine through, and returned the hinges to their former place. So much for moorland fences.

I mounted my bike and felt contented. I wondered how someone might interpret the footprints and wheel marks in the snow – there was a single wheeled track to the fence, a lot of untidiness around the gate and a wheeled single track leading from it. Once through, the terrain was terrible. I was crossing wild moorland, with my wheels bouncing and the machine bucking. I rode the bike in the style I'd now come to adopt, standing on the footrests and allowing it to buck and weave beneath me, trials style. I had a horror of falling off and breaking a leg, for no one would find me here. I would freeze to death, and for some two and a half miles, I carefully rode through snow which was smooth on the surface, but which concealed an alarming variety of pot-holes, clumps of heather, rocks and other hazards.

But I won. With my motorcycle and myself completely enveloped in frozen white, I managed to navigate that awesome moor. As I reached the distant edge of the moor, I saw to my right the three gleaming white balls of the Ballistic Missile Early Warning Station. They looked duck-egg blue against the pure white of the snow-covered backcloth, and dominated the surrounding moorland. The huge structures towered majestically above everything and looked surrealistic in this ancient moorland setting. The old and the new mingled in a fascinating manner.

Somewhere in the hollow which lay before the balls, but which was invisible to me due to the snow, there stood the sturdy moorland inn to which I was heading. I reached the main road and was pleased to note that traffic had passed this way. A snowplough had pushed its way through, and there was evidence of other vehicles. Sergeant Blaketon's message was therefore rather odd, because if a snowplough had forced its way along here, and if other traffic was passing, then it was difficult to understand how a bus load of businessmen had come to be marooned in the blizzard.

It would be about nine o'clock as I carefully descended the steep, twisting gradients of Moorcock Bank, and sure enough, a bus was standing on the car park of the inn. It bore a Bradford address, Bradford being some eighty-five miles away. Having parked my bike, I knocked on the door and a lady opened it; she smiled and her pretty face showed some surprise at my snow-clad appearance. I wondered if she knew I was a policeman – the POLICE legend across my helmet was totally obliterated.

'PC Rhea,' I announced, removing my gauntlets.

'Good heavens!' she stood back to allow me inside. 'What on earth are you doing here?'

'It's a long story,' I said, stamping the snow from my boots. It fell on to her doormat.

'Come in for a warm, for God's sake,' and she stepped back to permit me entry. The interior was comfortably warm, and I was shown into the bar area with its flagstone floor and smouldering peat fire. The place was full of men, some dozing and others sitting around quietly playing cards.

'Oh,' I said. 'Company?'

'Marooned,' she smiled. 'A bus load.'

I began to unbutton my stout clothing, my hands warm and pliable after the exercise of controlling the bike, and she asked, 'Coffee?'

'I'd love one.'

'I'm doing breakfast for that lot. Forty-two of them, bacon and eggs. How about you?'

At the mention of food my mouth began to water and I assured her that a delicious bacon and egg breakfast would be the best thing that could happen to me. She told me to remove my outer clothing and sit with the others. She'd call us into the dining-room when she was ready.

Some of the men glanced at me, and it was only when I peeled off the heavy jacket that they realised I was the law. I could see their renewed interest.

'What's this, Officer? A raid for drinking after time,

or before time?'

'No,' I struggled with the ungainly trousers and rubber boots and was soon standing with my back to the fire, warming my posterior and rubbing my hands. My face burned fiercely and my ears began to hurt as the sudden warmth made the blood course through them. I hadn't realised my extremities were so cold.

'Breakfast then?' a stout man smiled. 'You've called in for your breakfast?'

'I am going to have breakfast, as a matter of fact.' I looked at them. 'Are you the businessmen from Bradford?'

There was a long silence and then the stout man nodded. 'Aye,' he said. 'How come you know about us?'

'I'm searching for you,' I lied to make the matter seem more dramatic. 'There's a hue and cry out for you – there's reports of missing men snowed up in the North Yorkshire moors, men dying from starvation and exposure, buses falling down ravines and bodies all over…'

'Gerroff!' he laughed. 'Go on, what's up?'

'I'm out here on another job …'

'Not working? They haven't made you work out here, in all this snow, on a bloody motorbike?' One of them stood up and addressed me.

'They have. It's important,' I tried to explain without revealing national secrets.

'It must be – I'd have a strike at my factory if I even suggested such a thing,' and he sat down.

I tried to continue. 'I was called on my radio. Our Control Room said your bus was thought to have got stuck, and it was felt you might be here but they couldn't make contact because the telephone lines were down.'

'No, not down, Officer. We've taken the phone off the hook.'

'Off the hook!' I exploded. 'You mean I've come all this way ...'

'Look,' the stout man stood up and came towards me. 'We're businessmen, and we're always on call, always being rung up and wanted for some bloody thing or another. When we got here last night, for a drink, it was so nice and cosy that when the weather took a turn for the worse, we decided to stay. We took the telephone off the hook because we didn't want to be disturbed and we intended staying, didn't we, lads?'

'Aye,' came the chorus from the assembled group.

'This is our holiday, Officer. A sudden, unexpected and excellent holiday. Can you think of anything better than being snowed up in a moorland pub miles from civilisation? The landlord and his lady are marvellous and they've a stock of food that'll not get eaten unless they get crowds in. The beer's fine and we can play dominoes and cards to our hearts' content. We can drink all day because we're residents, and we've no worries about driving home or getting in late. Our wives will be happy enough that we're safe, and we'll stay here as long as we want, away from business pressures, telephones, secretaries, bank managers, problems and wives. We were going to ring today to tell them we're safe, but snowed up. Now you've gone and ruined it.'

'Sorry,' I said. 'As long as you're safe, my job is over. I'll report back by radio.'

'Don't say we're *not* snowed in, will you? I mean, we could leave now because the plough's been through, but we don't want to. Tell 'em we're safe, but stuck fast.'

'I'll simply radio to my Control to say you are here and you are all safe. Am I right in thinking none of you wants to be rescued?'

'No,' came the murmured chorus. 'For God's sake don't rescue us. Leave us, Officer. In a while, that telephone will mysteriously be reconnected and we'll convince our loved ones we're fine, sitting here in eight-foot drifts and suffering like hell, and then the telephone cables will come down again!'

'I get the message,' I said.

'Then join us for breakfast. Cereals, bacon, eggs and tomatoes and mushrooms, toast and hot coffee …'

I joined them. I couldn't refuse, not after my appetite-raising morning. They chattered about their meetings, their businesses, their twelve-hour days and hectic travelling, and I could see that this enforced holiday was perfect for them. They could relax totally, and I would not reveal this to anyone.

After breakfast, I told them I must leave. I got invitations to visit them and pocketed many address cards before buttoning up my motorcycle suit. Now it felt cold and damp, and the thought of leaving this warm place with its beams, open fires, smell of smoke and peat was awful. But I had a mission of national importance and I must not dally a moment longer.

As I fastened the zips and buttons, a young man in a fine suit and sleek blond hair came forward for a chat.

'You didn't come all this way just to find us, did you?'

'No.' I was honest. 'I've another job here.'

'I reckon it must be important to your people,' he said, puffing at a pipe, 'otherwise they wouldn't have made you risk life and limb by motorcycling here.'

'It is,' I confirmed, sliding my head into the cold helmet. I pulled the strap under my chin and it was wet with melted snow. I grimaced as I tightened it.

'Something to do with that chap that I saw crossing the moors, maybe?' he smiled knowingly.

'Aye.' I knew he'd seen my Russian!

'I saw him from that back bedroom,' he said. 'A tall chap dressed like a bloody Russian. Snow suit and big fur hat. He was crossing the moor on that track behind the pub.'

'What time?' I asked.

'Not long before you came,' he said. 'Quarter to nine, maybe.'

'Which way was he going?' I had fastened my chin strap and was ready to leave.

'Out towards the moor heights. I reckon he'd been sleeping in one of the outhouses of this place, Officer.'

'Thanks,' I said. 'I appreciate your interest.'

'And we appreciate your discretion,' he said.

I waved farewell to them, and thanked the lady for a superb breakfast. I'd been there well over an hour and was feeling fit and ready. I radioed a brief report to Control and merely confirmed their presence here. I said they were fit and well, with adequate food and warmth, and there was no risk to them.

To cut a long story short, I guided my faithful Francis Barnett towards the track in question and there I found a single trail of footprints. They emerged from an outbuilding close to the pub and it was easy to follow them in the snow. By now, the flakes had ceased falling and a wintry sun was trying to force a way through the heavy grey clouds. I thought again of Candlemas Day and wondered if the sun would shine.

It was said locally that, 'If Candlemas be dry and

29

fair, Half of winter's yet to come – and mair!'

Perhaps the rest of winter would be better than this?

After a mile and a half, the footprints wove erratically towards a grouse butt. I could see the boot marks etched clearly ahead of me as they climbed towards the lofty butt. Boris must be hiding there now! A grouse butt is like a three-sided square, it is made of stone with walls about four feet high. Grouse shooters lurk in there to blast at birds which are driven over their heads …

I decided to park and inform Control of this development. It seemed I had succeeded where others had failed. Upon receiving my message, I was instructed to await further orders. I waited for quarter of an hour, and this caused me to feel the cold for the first time. My feet, hands and face were icy and a bitter wind whipped the dry loose snow into small heaps and drifts. If the wind strengthened, this place could soon be well and truly isolated. Those businessmen might be there for days!

Then came the response from Control.

'Proceed to arrest,' I was ordered. I was a long way from the hiding man and decided to take the bike. At least, it would get me closer to him in a swift manner. I kicked it into life, and began to climb the rough track, with the wind biting into my face and driving loose snow into the goggles and among the engine parts. I wobbled in the fierce wind but kept my eyes on that distant grouse butt.

Suddenly, the man stood up. His head and trunk appeared above the rim of the butt as he stared in disbelief at my approach. Then he began to run. At that instant, a Land-Rover materialised from somewhere, having been hidden down a dip in the track and it also raced towards the fleeing Russian.

God, it was like something from a spy film! So those films were realistic after all!

I accelerated, but the snow-bound track caused the rear wheel to skid; I fought to maintain my motion and my balance as I saw the man running towards the Land-Rover. I was roaring towards them both. I had to get there first, this being my first major arrest. A spy!

I stood on the footrests and allowed the little bike to buck and roar beneath me as I closed in; now I could see the fellow's eyes beneath his furry white hat and the Land-Rover was a similar distance at the far side of him. It was neck and neck. I must win! I couldn't let the nation down at a time of such need. I would have to abandon my bike, I would have to leap off as I neared him, and allow the machine to fall into the snow, but I *must* make this arrest. For the country's sake, for the Chief Constable's sake, for my own sake.

I climbed the rising ground as the Land-Rover hurtled towards me with clouds of snow rising behind. The fugitive moved closer towards it. I was only yards away; I could see his thick leather boots, his snow suit, his furry hat ...

He was mine. I had him!

But he wasn't, and I hadn't.

The Land-Rover did not stop at him; instead it came directly for me, with its rear wheels skidding violently and the front ones bucking against the rough terrain. God, I was going to be killed!

I swerved aside; I tore at the handlebars and yanked the front wheel to one side, but I was too late. The motorcycle toppled over as the heavy wing of the Land-Rover clipped the handlebars. I was thrown right off. I rolled clear and felt myself falling down a hillside. I curled up into a protective ball, with my helmet, suit and gloves providing ideal protection as I gathered speed down a snow-filled, bracken-covered and heather-clad moorland slope. I could hear the victorious Land-Rover roaring away, and my motorcycle engine had stopped somewhere out of sight.

I came to rest at the bottom, shaken but not hurt. The heather, with its springy tough stalks, had bounced me down that hillside like a ball, and when I got to my feet, I saw that the Land-Rover had stopped further along. Several faces peered at me and I waved my fist at them.

They waved back, and as I started to climb the slope, tugging at heather roots for support, they vanished over the horizon.

I had lost my Russian.

Six weeks later, we were in a classroom for a one-day course. The subject was 'Liaison with the C.I.D.' A detective inspector from Headquarters was laying down the rules about communication between departments, and liaison between officers and men.

'Exercise Moorjock was a perfect example of confusion,' he said.

Was that an exercise? I thought it was the real thing! I'd given my all on that occasion, I'd risked my life and my limbs!

'There was no communication, no liaison. We shot a film of the exercise to highlight some of the problems,' he said. 'It speaks for itself.'

And when the lights went out and the film hit the screen, I saw myself riding towards the camera; I saw the pseudo-Russian waiting for me, and I saw myself tumbling down a moorland hillside in a cloud of winter snow.

I could not forget those Candlemas Day events, but

did remember the old Yorkshire saying, 'Look for nowt in February – and you'll get it.'

Chapter 2

'This only is the witchcraft I have us'd'
WILLIAM SHAKESPEARE (1564–1616) *Othello*

'RHEA? ARE YOU THERE?'

It was Sergeant Blaketon and I was retrieving a heap of files from the floor of my office. I had lifted the telephone to answer and had dislodged a heap of paperwork with the cable.

'Sorry, Sergeant,' I responded. 'Yes, I'm here.'

'Get yourself out to Ellersfield,' he instructed me. 'Go and see a Miss Katherine Hardwick of Oak Crag Cottage. She's got a complaint to make.'

'What sort of complaint, Sergeant?' I was still struggling to hold the telephone with one hand and pick up the files with the other. It would have been easier to leave them on the floor, but they annoyed me.

'Mischief makers,' he said. 'She's being plagued by somebody from the village, one of the lads by the sound of it.'

'Kids!' I snorted. 'What's he doing to her?'

'Daft things really, knocking on her door when she's in bed and running away before she opens it, tapping on the window when she's sitting alone, pinching tomatoes from her greenhouse and cutting the tops off all her cabbages. That sort of thing. Nuisances, Rhea, nothing but bloody nuisances.'

'Is she a regular complainer?' I asked him.

'No, she's not. She's a decent hard-working woman who lives alone and she earns her keep by growing flowers and vegetables, or doing odd jobs for the folk of the area.'

'I'm on my way,' I said.

'Good. It'll keep you quiet for the rest of the morning. Anything else to report?'

'Nothing, Sergeant, it's all quiet.' It was extremely quiet. My beat had lacked any real trouble or serious incident for the past six weeks, but this lull may have been due to the weather. The winter snows and gales tended to keep people away from the moors and its range of villages, but now the spring had arrived, my workload would surely increase. Life was beginning anew, and I wondered if this lad's activities with Miss Hardwick were a sign of rising sap.

I departed from my hilltop house on my trusty Francis Barnett, clad up to the eyeballs in my winter suit, goggles, helmet and gloves. The crisp air contained a definite chill, but the brightness of the morning and the clarity of the views across the valleys and hills were truly magnificent. I was faced with a journey of some eighteen miles each way, and braced myself for the long, cold ride. There would be none of the gymnastics I'd enjoyed during Exercise Moorjock.

I dropped into Ashfordly, rode through the sleepy market town and out towards Eltering before turning high into the moorlands which overlooked Ryedale. Here, the roads were reduced to tracks and I marvelled at the new growth blossoming from the depths of dead vegetation. The grass was showing a brighter green, new leaves were bursting from apparently lifeless stems and animals romped in the fields, glad to be rid of

35

winter's burden and looking forward to the joy of spring.

My machine and I climbed across the ranging hills with their acres of smooth moorland, and I enjoyed the limitless vista of steep slopes, craggy outcrops and deep valleys. They combined to produce a beauty of landscape seldom found elsewhere. And there was not a person about. I had the moors to myself.

True, I did pass one or two cars, and in the villages I noted ladies going about their daily shopping or cleaning their cottage windows, but beyond the inhabited areas, there was a sense of isolation that was intriguing. It was like entering a deserted world, an area devoid of people and houses but full of living things like birds and plants and animals. In some respects, it was like a fairyland, with wisps of mist hanging near the valley floors and shafts of strong sunlight piercing the density of the man-made forests and natural woodland. The smell of peace and tranquillity was everywhere.

Ellersfield lay snug in one of these deep valleys, a cluster of stone-built houses nestling at the head of the dale. All had thatched roofs, and they were sturdy dwellings, somewhat squat in appearance but constructed to withstand the fierce winters of the moors. Oak Crag Cottage stood at the far end as I rode into the community, using a road which ended in a rough cart track as it climbed steeply on to the moors before vanishing among the heather.

It was a neatly kept house. The thatch was carefully maintained and an evergreen hedge acted as a boundary between the cottage and the track by which it stood. The wooden gate was painted a fresh green and bore the name of the house in white letters. I parked the motorcycle on its stand and opened the gate, walking clumsily in my ungainly suit.

The house had three windows along its front with two attic windows above, all with tiny panes of glass and all neatly picked out in fresh white paint. I knocked on the door and waited. There was no reply.

I tried again, with the same result, and guessed the lady of the house must be around because she'd called in the police to solve her problem. As policemen are wont to do, I moved away from the front door and walked along the sandstone flags to the rear. At the back was a long, flat garden with sheds and poultry runs, and I saw a woman repairing a wire netting fence at the far end.

'Hello!' I shouted.

She stood up, placing a hand on her back to indicate some form of backache. She smiled a welcome.

'Oh, hello. Is it the police?'

'Yes,' I confirmed, realising my gear made me look like a refugee from the Royal Flying Corps of World War I. 'I'm PC Rhea from Aidensfield.'

She came towards me looking pleased as she removed some rubber gloves. She wore a headscarf which almost concealed her face, and I wondered if she was pretty.

'Katherine Hardwick,' she introduced herself. 'Miss,' she added as an afterthought. 'I'm sorry to trouble you, but I thought I'd better put an official stop to my unwelcome visitor.'

'You did exactly the right thing,' I endeavoured to comfort her a little. 'You know who it is?'

She shook her head and said, 'Come inside, I'll make a coffee. You'll have a coffee?'

'There's nothing I'd like more.' The spring air had

given me a healthy appetite and thirst, and she led me through a rear door into the interior of her cottage.

It was very dark inside and I noticed the rear windows were very small, so typical of these moorland houses. They aided warmth and security in the harshest of weathers. Her kitchen was a long, narrow room with modern electric equipment, but she led me through and into her lounge.

As the kettle boiled, she settled on a Windsor chair and smiled pleasantly, removing the headscarf as she talked. She was a very tall woman, with an almost angular body and she appeared to be shapeless beneath her rough country clothes. She had a long overcoat which was all tattered and greasy, corduroy trousers and wellington boots, but as the headscarf came away, I saw that her face was beautifully smooth and pink. Her eyes were bright and alert, her teeth excellent and her hair as black as night, cut short but not severely so. I estimated her age to be less than forty, but probably beyond thirty-five. She was very attractive in a rural way, and I wondered what she'd be like in an evening dress or a summer frock. Did she ever wear nice clothes, I wondered.

The kettle began to whistle and she took off her old coat to reveal a well-proportioned figure clad in a rose-coloured sweater.

She vanished into her kitchen and returned with two cups of steaming coffee, a jug of fresh cream and a basin of sugar. Some homemade fruit cake and ginger biscuits adorned the tray.

'This is lovely,' I congratulated her. 'You shouldn't have bothered.'

'It's nice to get visitors, and besides, it's 'lowance time anyway. Now, Mr Rhea, did your sergeant tell you what this is about?'

'Somebody's playing pranks, being a nuisance, frightening you?'

'That's about it, Mr Rhea. I'm not one for calling the police, I usually sort out my own troubles but I felt this one ought to receive the weight of the law. There's other folks who live alone up here, you see, and some are elderly. I don't want them terrified.'

'There's not many folk live out here is there?' I sipped my hot coffee. It was delicious.

'Seventy or so, it's not many,' she confirmed.

'You have an idea who's doing these stupid things?'

'I have,' she said, 'and I've warned him off. He says it's not him, but things keep happening.'

'Such as?' I wanted her to tell me more.

'It's nothing serious. Last back end, for example, he opened my greenhouse door after I'd closed it for the night and the cold air ruined some young plants and flowers. He's let the hens out of their run and they ruined my garden when I was in Middlesbrough for the day; he knocks on windows and runs off when I'm alone in the house. One day, he cut all the heads off my cabbages and ruined them, and another time took the seat off my bike and threw it into a field.'

'Are you frightened?'

'No,' she said. 'No, I'm not frightened. It's just a bloody nuisance, Mr Rhea, and I wonder if he's doing it to others in Ellersfield, others who are too shy or old to report it. People are shy out here, you know, they don't like making a fuss.'

'I know,' I knew enough about the stolid Yorkshire character to fully understand her remarks. 'Right, who is it?'

'It's a youth called Ted Agar,' she said, with never a

doubt in her voice.

'You've seen him doing these things?' I put to her, enjoying the cake.

'No,' she admitted. 'But it's him.'

'How can you be so sure?' I had to ask.

She hesitated and I wondered if I had touched a sensitive area. I allowed her to take her time before replying. She drank a deep draught from her cup.

'Mr Rhea, I'm a woman and I live alone. I'm thirty-six, and I'm not bad looking. Ted's been pestering me to go out with him – to the pictures, for walks, over to Scarborough for a Sunday trip, that sort of thing. He's only a child, Mr Rhea, a lad in his early twenties I'd say. I've turned him down every time and these things started to go on.'

'Over what period?'

'Maybe a year, no longer.'

'Is he a local lad?' I asked.

'Not really. He came from Eltering, looking for farm work and the Atkinsons took him on.'

'Atkinsons?'

'Dell Farm, at the bottom of the hill on your way in. That big spot with double iron gates.'

'I know it,' I smiled. 'OK. Well, Miss Hardwick, I can have words with him for you. I can threaten him with court action – we could proceed against him for conduct likely to cause a breach of the peace. That way, we could have him bound over to be of good behaviour, and if he did it again, he'd be fined or sent to a detention centre of some kind.'

'I don't want to take him to court. A warning from you would be fine,' she said. 'I know he'll think I'm using a sledgehammer to crack a little nut, but he won't stop when I ask him. I thought a word from you might help.'

'I'll speak to him. Will he be in now, at the Atkinsons'?'

'He'll be about the premises somewhere,' she acknowledged.

I drained my coffee and stood up. 'I'll let you know how I get on – I'll come straight back.'

Before I left, I briefly admired her home. The kitchen was a real gem. The fireplace, for example, had an old stone surround with a black-leaded Yorkist range, complete with sliding hooks for pans, and a side oven. It was set in an inglenook and to the right was a wooden partition beyond which was a passage into a further series of rooms.

'It's a fascinating house,' I observed.

'It's an old cruck house,' she explained. 'It used to be a longhouse, that's a farm house where the family lived at one end and the cattle at the other. The living quarters were warmed by the animals as they wintered next door. The crucks are like tree trunks, and they support the building. It's very old – I couldn't hazard a date.'

'Did you move out here?'

'No,' she smiled. 'It's been in our family for generations. There's always been a Hardwick here, as long as anybody knows.'

I walked around the spacious kitchen, and expressed delight at the ancient woodwork, so crude but effective, and then I noticed the carved wooden post at the outer end of the partition. I ran my hands down it, fingering the delicate workmanship.

'This is nice – what's the carving? The X-mark?'

'That's a witch post,' she informed me. 'Lots of houses had them installed.'

'What's it for?' I had never come across this type of

41

thing before.

'They were built into many houses in this area to protect the occupants against witches,' she smiled. 'They date from the seventeenth century mostly, but I've never dated ours.'

'Was witchcraft practised here?' I was intrigued by this decorative post.

'A good number of old women were reputed to be witches,' she said. 'They were supposed to make the milk go sour, or cause the fruit not to ripen – stuff like that. Nuisances more than anything. There wasn't your dancing naked bits or rituals in lonely woods. They were just old ladies who terrified the superstitious locals and got blamed when things went wrong. Those posts protected the inhabitants against them.'

After my obvious interest in her house, she showed me the rest of the layout of the fascinating building with its nooks and crannies, beamed bedroom ceilings, sandstone floors and rubble walls. It was a house of considerable age, albeit modernised to meet her modest needs.

I left my motorcycle near her gate as I walked down the steep hill to Dell Farm. This was a neat homestead with freshly painted gates and a scrupulously tidy farmyard. I made for the house, although I could hear activity in one of the outbuildings, knocked on the door and waited. At my second knock, a woman's voice shouted, 'Come in, the door's open.'

I entered a spacious farm kitchen with hams hanging from the ceiling and the smell of new bread heavy in the air. An old lady sat in a chair beside a roaring log fire. I think I must have aroused her from her slumbers.

'And who might you be?' she demanded, looking me up and down.

'PC Rhea,' I said. 'The policeman. From Aidensfield.'

'You're a bit off your area, aren't you?' she quizzed me sharply, her keen grey eyes alert and bright. I reckoned she was well into her seventies, or even older.

'Not any more. Now we've got motorcycles, we go further than we did on bikes. We share the area.'

'You'll have come for our Reg, have you? Summat to do with his guns, is it?'

'Are you Mrs Atkinson?'

'I am, but Reg is my son. He's the boss here – I'm just an old lady who lives in. Our Reg's wife, that's young Mrs Atkinson, is down at Ashfordly, shopping. Susan, that is.'

'It's really young Agar I want to see,' I explained.

'Why would you want to see him, then? He's not in trouble, is he?'

'No,' I said, 'but I hear he's been making a pest of himself.'

'Pest? What sort of pest?'

I provided brief details of his alleged misbehaviour and she listened intently, leaving me standing in the middle of the floor. She smiled fleetingly, and when I'd finished, she said, 'Lads will be lads, it'll be due to his sap rising, Mr Rhea!'

'I agree it's nothing serious, Mrs Atkinson, but his behaviour is unnerving for Miss Hardwick.'

'Hardwick, did you say?' she threw the question at me, with those eyes flashing brightly.

'Yes, up at Oak Crag Cottage.'

'Then she ought to know better than to bring you in, should that one,' the old lady said. 'Fancy bringing you all the way in for a trifling thing like that … she ought to be ashamed.'

43

'It's not nice, Mrs Atkinson, having unknown lads making nuisances of themselves when you're a woman living alone. I don't mind coming out to help put a stop to it.'

'Nay, it's not that, Mr Rhea, it's that woman. Hardwick. It's the first time I've come across a Hardwick woman that couldn't sort things out by herself.'

'Why?' I asked, intrigued. Katherine Hardwick seemed a perfectly ordinary young woman.

'They're witches,' she said with all seriousness. 'All Hardwick women are witches.'

I laughed. 'Witches?' I said, thinking she was joking.

'You'll have heard of Nan Hardwick, haven't you? Awd Nan Hardwick, who was a witch in these hills years ago?'

'No,' I had to confess.

'Then just you listen, young man,' and she motioned me to a wooden chair. I sat down, interested to hear her story. I knew that old ladies tended to ramble and reminisce, but Mrs Atkinson appeared totally in control of her senses, and deadly serious too. She spoke with disarming frankness.

After leaning forward in her chair and eyeing me carefully, she unravelled her extraordinary story. She was in her late eighties, she told me by way of introduction, and then related the fable of Awd Nan Hardwick. She was a witch whose notoriety was widespread in the North Yorkshire moors when Mrs Atkinson was a young girl; everyone for miles around knew Awd Nan.

She told me a story about a farmer's wife who was expecting a baby. One afternoon, Awd Nan chanced to pass the house and called in for some food and a rest as she was several miles from home. She asked for a 'shive o' bread and a pot o' beer'. The food was readily given to her and during the conversation, she let it be known she was aware of the young wife's condition. She wished the girl well and said, 'Thoo'll have a lad afoor morning, and thoo'll call him Tommy, weeant thoo?'

The girl replied that she and her husband had already decided to name the child John if it was a boy, but Awd Nan replied, 'Aye, mebbe thoo has, but thoo'd best call him Tommy. And now, Ah'll say goodbye,' and off she went.

Both the husband and the girl were determined to name the child John, and later that evening, the prospective father drove a pony and trap across the moors to collect his sister-in-law. She had offered to help with the birth. Three miles from the farm, he had to cross a small bridge, but the horse stopped twenty yards before reaching it and steadfastly refused to move. Try as he might, the farmer could not persuade the animal to proceed, so he tried to leave his seat on the trap. To his horror, he found he was unable to move. In his words, 'Ah was ez fast as owt.'

Eventually he concluded that Awd Nan had put a spell on him and shouted into the air, 'Now, Nan, what's thoo after? Is this tha work?'

To his amazement, a voice apparently from thin air replied, 'Thoo'll call that bairn Tommy, weearn't tha?'

The husband, still determined to select his own name, shouted back, 'Ah'll call ma lad what Ah wants. Ah weearn't change it for thoo or for all t'Nan devils in this country.'

'Then thoo'll stay where thoo is until t'bairn's born

and t'mother dies,' came the horrifying response.

The poor young farmer was placed in a terrible dilemma. He could not move his pony and trap, nor could he climb from the seat, and he was faced with the death of his dear wife, all for the sake of a lad's name. As he sat transfixed, he reasoned it all out, and decided there was an element of uncertainty because the child might be a girl. For that reason, he capitulated. He agreed to call the child Tommy if it was a boy. And at that, he found the horse could move and he went on his way.

My storyteller did not tell me whether the child was a boy, and I did not ask in case she was talking about her own ancestors, but she went on to relate more stories of Awd Nan Hardwick, all showing belief in the curious power of these local witches.

As I listened, it was evident that she believed the stories, and I could imagine her family relating these yarns as the children gathered around a blazing fire during the long dark evenings of a moorland winter.

'Is Katherine Hardwick a descendant of Awd Nan?' I asked.

'She is,' the lady nodded her grey head seriously. 'All those Hardwick women were witches, and she's no better. Mark my words, young man.'

'What sort of things does she do then?'

'Turns milk sour if she comes in the house, makes folks ill by looking at them. Little things like that, like her mother and the other women folk did. Milk would never come to butter if a Hardwick was around.'

'Is that why you said she could sort out her own trouble with this mischief maker?' I asked.

'Aye,' she said, 'any witch worth her salt could sort out that kind of trouble.'

'But with all due respect, Mrs Atkinson, witches don't exist ...'

'Balderdash!' she snorted. 'Do you know what they did in a situation like this? When folks upset them, angered them, scandalised them?'

I shook my head.

'The witch took a pigeon, Mr Rhea, a wild pigeon, a wood stoggie we used to call 'em. They made pigeon pie, but they took the heart out and stuck pins into it, into the heart that is. They put as many pins in as they could, lots and lots, and then put the heart into a tin and cooked it. Then they put it near the door, out of reach of cats and things, out of sight.'

'And?'

'Well, it made the mischief maker want to apologise for what he'd done. He went to the house and made his peace. It allus works, Mr Rhea.' She spoke her final words in the present tense.

'And you think Katherine should do that?' I put the direct question.

'Nay, lad, Ah didn't say that. Ah said she *could* do that, because her previous women folk did that sort o' thing. If she wants to bring you fellers in, then that's her business.' She spoke those words with an air of finality.

'Is Ted Agar in, Mrs Atkinson? I ought to talk to him while I'm here.'

'Try those sheds at the bottom of our yard, he's down there fettling t'tractor.'

'Thanks – and thanks for the story of Awd Nan.'

'It's true,' she said as I left the warmth of the kitchen to seek Ted Agar. I found him working on the tractor. He had the plugs out and was cleaning some parts with a wire brush, his face wrapped with

47

concentration as I entered the spacious building.

'Ted Agar?' I spoke his name as I walked in.

He glanced up from his work and smiled at me. 'Aye, that's me.'

'I'm PC Rhea from Aidensfield,' I announced, thinking this would give him notice of the reason for my presence.

He continued to work, acknowledging me with a curt nod of his curly black head. He was about twenty-two or three, I guessed, a sturdy youth in dirty overalls and heavy hobnailed boots. His face was round and weathered with a hint of mischief written into his smile.

'Summat up, is it?' he asked.

'Have you been annoying Katherine Hardwick?' I decided to put the matter straight to him. 'Playing jokes on her, messing up her garden and so on?'

'Me? No,' he said without batting an eyelid, and without stopping his work.

'Somebody has,' I said. 'She's upset and if I catch the person, it'll mean court.'

'It's not me,' he said firmly, furiously rubbing at a piece of rusty metal with the wire brush.

'Then don't do it,' I said, leaving him. I felt it would be a waste of time, pressing him further. Denials of this kind rarely produced anything beyond those words, so I left him to his maintenance work. I poked my head around the kitchen door to inform old Mrs Atkinson that I'd found him, and said I was leaving. If Agar was the culprit, I felt my brief visit would halt his unwelcome attentions.

I walked back up the village to my motorcycle and popped over to Katherine Hardwick's house to explain my action. I went around to the back but she was not in the garden, and I noticed the kitchen door was open. I knocked and stepped inside a couple of paces, shouting 'Miss Hardwick? Are you there?'

There was no reply, so I continued to shout as I entered the kitchen. Her lunch was in the course of preparation, so she must be around. I called again, 'Miss Hardwick?'

'Upstairs,' she shouted. 'Who is it?'

'The policeman,' I shouted back. 'PC Rhea.'

'Oh, I'll be down in a minute,' she replied. 'Sit down.'

I sat on a kitchen chair, holding my crash helmet in my hands. And as I waited, my eyes ranged across the half-prepared meal. A pigeon lay on the kitchen table, plucked clean except for its head. Its innards lay beside it, having been expertly gutted and I saw the tiny heart set aside from the other giblets. There was a small tin beside the heart, and a pin cushion, thick with pins and needles. I thought of Mrs Atkinson and her tales of Awd Nan …

'Hello,' she returned, smiling broadly. 'Sorry, I was upstairs. I was changing out of my working clothes, I'm going into Eltering this afternoon.'

'I just popped in to say I've spoken to young Agar,' I announced. 'He denied making mischief, but I'm convinced it was him. I warned him about the consequences of repeating any mischief at your house, so I reckon we've seen the last of him. If he does come back, or if anybody else starts those tricks, let me know.'

'It's most kind of you, Mr Rhea. I really appreciate your help.'

After some small talk, I left her to her cooking, my brain striving to recall the details of Mrs Atkinson's story. It was definitely a pigeon's heart on that table, and the pin cushion was so conveniently positioned next to it …

Three days later, my telephone rang.

'Is that PC Rhea?' asked a woman's voice.

'Speaking.'

'It's Katherine Hardwick,' the voice told me. 'You called the other day, about young Agar.'

'That's right,' I recalled. 'Has he been troubling you again?'

'On the contrary,' there was a smile in her voice. 'He's been to apologise. He said he did it for a lark, but didn't realise the upset he would cause. I've accepted his apology, Mr Rhea, so there won't be any need for further action, will there?'

'No,' I agreed. 'No, that's all. There will be no court action. Thanks for ringing.'

I replaced the phone and reckoned the previous generations of Hardwick women would be very proud of their Katherine.

Happily for the Hardwick women and those of their ilk, the Witchcraft Act of 1735 had been repealed, albeit not until 1951.

England had had a long history of cruelty and antagonism towards old ladies who were regarded as witches, and before the 1735 Act, witchcraft had been a capital offence. The last judicial execution for witchcraft possibly occurred at Huntingdon in 1716, when a woman and her nine-year-old daughter were hanged, and the last recorded committal was at Leicester in 1717 when an old woman and her son were charged with casting spells, possessing familiars and being able to change their shapes.

It was not until 1951, however, that witches were safe from prosecution in England, and the statute which brought about this change was the Fraudulent Mediums

Act, 1951.

The provision of that Act which was of interest to the police was Section 1. It created the offence of acting as a spiritualistic medium or using telepathy, clairvoyance or other similar powers with intent to deceive, or when so acting using any fraudulent device when it is proved that the person so acted for reward.

Those who reckon they can perform miracles of this kind purely for entertainment need have no worries, but those who seek to make money from their so-called powers can expect a file of their activities to be sent to the Director of Public Prosecutions and they can also claim right of trial by jury if things go that far.

In the bucolic bliss of North Yorkshire's Ryedale, I hardly expected to consider a prosecution under the Fraudulent Mediums Act of 1951, but my eyes were opened at the Annual Whist Drive and Jumble Sale held in Aidensfield Village Hall. This was an early event in the year, the social occasion of the spring equinox, when everyone in the village took mountains of junk for someone else to buy, and obliged by buying mountains of someone else's junk in return. Thus the junk of the village did a tour of the households and much money passed hands for worthy causes such as the church steeple fund, the old age pensioners' outing fund, the R.S.P.C.A. and other animal charities, including charities for children. Much money was made, and much junk was disposed of, to be returned for re-sale after a suitable period in someone's home.

The system was illustrated perfectly when my tiny daughter purchased for one shilling a box camera I had given away five years earlier for another jumble sale not far away. She bore her purchase proudly home, only to find the shutter didn't work because it was bent. She kept it and donated it to the sale the following year. I imagine that camera is still being bought and sold and I'm sure it now qualifies as an antique. If I see it around, I might buy it as a keepsake.

Because of the large volume of traffic expected at the function, Sergeant Blaketon telephoned and instructed me to perform duty outside the hall that Saturday afternoon. I had to control the crowds, prevent indiscriminate parking and keep an eye open for pickpockets and other villains. I parked the five cars without much ado, I controlled the perambulating crowds which swarmed the street, and kept vigil for local villains. I was not unduly busy.

The only villain likely to make an appearance was Claude Jeremiah Greengrass, and I was somewhat surprised and, I dare admit, disappointed, when he failed to put in his anticipated attendance. Claude Jeremiah liked jumble sales because he bought most of his clothes and furniture from such places, and I know he managed to earn a little extra cash by re-selling items of interest. I liked him there because his presence gave me work – I had to keep an eye on him to stop him stealing things.

With the grand opening neatly performed at 2.30 p.m. by the vicar's wife, and with my public order and parking duties enforced without incident, I entered the hall for a survey of pickpockets and ne'er-do-wells. Mary had brought the children, all four of them, and our family formed a crowd in its own right. The Rhea procession had entered some time earlier, and satisfied that crimes were not being committed, I looked about to see what I could purchase. The tiny hall was full, a pleasing sight, with nice people making faces at each other and complimenting the ladies for baking cakes, mending old clothes and manning stalls.

I found Mary and our little entourage and helped her guide the family around the stands, examining vintage baby clothes, looking at battered furnishings and cracked crockery, and deciding not to buy anything. And then I spotted the fortune teller.

This was a new idea. As my eyes settled on the ornate tent in a corner in front of the stage, I found it most impressive. The tent had the appearance of a small Arabian structure, circular in shape with a tall centre pole and flags flying from the top. The drapes were open down the front and the mysterious interior was coloured deep purple enhanced by golden curtains with a green centre support. In front of the opening was a table, also covered with purple and gold drapes, and upon the table was a crystal ball and several other implements used by a gypsy fortune teller. A large notice pinned to the tent told us this was Gypsy Rose Lee.

Behind the ball sat the gypsy herself. She was a small woman with a deeply tanned face, most of which was smothered by a veil which covered the nose and mouth. Her head was swathed in brilliant silken bands which cascaded down the rear of her neck, and her voluminous sleeves billowed as she sat before the crystal ball. Her hands were heavy with jewellery, and a tiny bowl of incense burned inside the tent, sending a strong aroma about the hall.

It was a most impressive display, and I watched with fascination because every woman in the place seemed to want her fortune told. I heard the chink of silver as money changed hands, and was surprised to see the growing queue of women, all eager to have their palms read or their fortunes told for the princely sum of five shillings.

I was kept fairly busy during the sale. Children got lost, people misplaced belongings, old ladies lost keys and purses, some teenage lads became a shade too boisterous and an exploding fuse put all the lights out. Mary and the children appeared to enjoy the occasion, but left early because the youngsters had exhausted themselves as only tots can. I helped Mary take the family up to my house on the hill and returned to the Hall to be present at the conclusion of this momentous event.

By five o'clock it was all over. The cake stall was deserted, and only crumbs remained; the soft drinks now comprised many crates of drained bottles, and the assorted stalls of junk had little left, other than the annual complement of totally unsaleable rubbish. This would come out again next year. I chatted to Miss Jenks, the secretary and treasurer of the Village Hall Committee and expressed my pleasure at a well-conducted event.

'Thank you, Mr Rhea.' She was a retired school-teacher of the old kind, stern and humourless. 'We have done well, but then we always do.'

'What's the profit? Do we know yet?'

'Not yet, but I imagine it will be around the £150 mark, an excellent result. It is going to the church steeple fund this year.'

'I liked the gypsy idea – a real novelty,' I nodded in the direction of the heavily-clad woman who was demolishing her tent and packing her fortune-telling impedimenta.

'Yes, it was a good crowd puller. She rang me rather late to be mentioned in our posters and advertisements, but word got around.'

'Who is she?'

'Gypsy Rose Lee,' smiled Miss Jenks. 'The real one, the one you see at Blackpool in the summer. She rang to ask if she could hire space from us.'

'Hire space?'

'Yes, she rang me and asked what I'd charge to rent a corner of the room.'

'And what did you say?' I asked gently.

'I said we didn't hire space, but if she really wanted to come and entertain us, she could give us ten per cent of her takings, and they would go to the steeple fund.'

'And she could keep the rest?'

'Yes, the committee felt it was a nice idea. I telephoned them all when I got the request, and Gypsy Rose rang back for our decision. We all agreed, Mr Rhea ...' her voice trailed away as she explained this to me. 'Oh dear, I say, I haven't broken the law, have I?'

'No,' I smiled. 'No, but the gypsy might have. If she's been taking money for herself, by professing to tell fortunes with the intention of deceiving the public, then she might have committed a criminal offence.'

'Oh, Mr Rhea, it's all a bit of innocent fun.'

I would have agreed had it not been for my recollection of lots of cash dropping into the palm of that gypsy. If every woman had had her fortune told this afternoon, with some children, that gypsy would have reaped a fortune. I made a hasty calculation in my head and reckoned she'd collected about £70. If she gave £7 of that to charity, it left a huge profit – over £60 – more than a month's wages for the average man.

The tent had by this time been reduced to a pile of flimsy material which was being packed into a large suitcase, along with the ornate pole. That was now in short sections. The crystal ball had gone, and the other materials were in a large leather bag. Only the woman remained and she was still in her heavy fancy dress. I found that rather odd. Why hadn't she changed into everyday clothes?

I stared at her, busy with her packing, and the provisions of the Fraudulent Mediums Act 1951 flickered from the dark recesses of my memory. She had taken money …

I stood alone, racking my brains, as Miss Jenks counted piles of money into a tin at my side. I was vaguely aware that the gypsy woman was heading for the cloakroom, no doubt to change out of her ceremonial dress.

She walked across the floor before us, weaving expansively through the rubbish which remained, and she vanished into the cloakrooms. I chattered to Miss Jenks for a few minutes, and then decided I needed to use the gents. I made for the cloakroom too. One of the cubicles was occupied, showing the 'Engaged' sign. And on the floor, I found a pile of flimsy silk and chiffon. I heard a window click …

I rushed out and ran down the alley at the side of the village hall. I was just in time to see Claude Jeremiah Greengrass, with his face the colour of chocolate, squeezing out of the gents' toilet window.

'Hello, Claude Jeremiah,' I beamed. 'Going far?'

He said nothing. There is very little one can say when one is caught climbing out of a gents' toilet window with one's face coloured chocolate, and with ornate earrings dangling from one's aching lobes. I seized his shoulders and hauled him through, placing him squarely on the ground before me. His wizened, pinched and elfin face twitched as I said, 'Pockets – open them all up, turn them out.'

Still without speaking, he obeyed. To give the fellow

his due, when he was caught red-handed, he was most co-operative. He produced £62 10s 0d in cash, and there was a further £5 in his wallet.

'The wallet money's mine, Mr Rhea,' he said, and I believed him. The other was in a separate pocket, and I knew enough of my local villain's behaviour to realise he'd keep today's cash takings separate from the other.

Standing there in the back alley, I chanted the provisions of the Fraudulent Mediums Act to him and told him he was being reported for contravening its provisions. I felt sure the Director of Public Prosecutions would be fascinated to learn of this incident at our Jumble Sale, and firmly gripping Claude's collar, I steered him back into the room to face Miss Jenks.

'Miss Jenks,' I said, 'this is your gypsy. Claude Jeremiah Greengrass to be precise, and he has a donation to make to your charity. Isn't that right, Claude?'

I shook his collar.

'Yes, Mr Rhea,' and I handed her the money.

She was sufficiently fast-thinking to appreciate the situation, and I noted the quick smile as she looked at the abandoned suitcases and unpacked tent.

'There was the question of rent for that space, Miss Jenks,' I said. 'Mr Greengrass and I had a discussion outside, and we agreed that £5 was a reasonable sum for the afternoon. Mr Greengrass will be happy to oblige, I'm sure.'

'But Mr Rhea, there's all that money ...'

'Rent, Claude, or it's a file to the D.P.P., my lad ...'

'Yes, Mr Rhea.'

He pulled out his wallet, extracted five pound notes and gingerly handed them to Miss Jenks. She smiled, issued a receipt and pushed the cash into a money box. 'Mr Greengrass, this is most generous. I do believe this jumble sale's profits are the best we've ever had, thanks to you. I must make a note in the minutes. Maybe you'd come again next year?'

'I'm sure he will, Miss Jenks, and on the same terms, Claude Jeremiah?'

And, as we say in the Force, he made no reply.

Chapter 3

'Oh, dry the starting tear, for they were heavily
insured.'

SIR W.S. GILBERT (1836–1911)

ONE OF MY GREATEST delights was to ride the sturdy
little Francis Barnett across the wild acres of stirring
moorland which lie to the north of Aidensfield. Lofty
roads and rough tracks interlace across the more
accessible regions of the heathered heights while
prominent summits dot the horizons to mark the
extremities of the more remote parts of the unpopulated
portions. But even those far-flung borders conceal
beauty and mystery, and are worthy of exploration.

Many is the time I have parked my little machine on
the roadside at some eminent outcrop, to sit and admire
the panoramic spread below. Mile after mile of
uninhabited land, some of it moorland but much of it
comprising green valleys, can be seen from countless
vantage points. A succession of artists have attempted
to capture the expansive attraction of the moors and
dales, but few have painted a memorable reproduction.
One or two have captured the exquisite purple of the
heather, and some have caught the sheer enormity of
the emptiness within the ranging hills. A true picture of
the landscape eludes many. The hardiness of the

residents has also defied interpretation by striving artists and the region is virtually ignored by novelists.

I have often considered myself fortunate to be paid a salary for touring these moors and valleys, whereas visitors pay substantially to explore them. That is the chief perquisite of the country constable in North Yorkshire.

But if the countryside is replete with attractions, then so are the people who scrape a living from these hills. Sheep farming dominates but in the lowland districts, the farmers manage to eke out a living through versatility and hard work. Few of them take a holiday or even a day off because their work and responsibility makes full-time demands upon them and their families. Because their work is their entire life, they are utterly happy and deeply content, a rare thing in any era.

On my visits to the more distant areas, I made regular calls at the lonely farms. These were chiefly to inspect stock registers or to renew or verify firearms certificates, and it meant I was known to every farmer in the district. The homesteads comprised every kind of farm from the huge, multi-owned premises run by a manager, to the tiny single-cow farm with a few hens and pigs, but which somehow maintained a man and his wife.

I learned to negotiate cattle grids, unmade tracks, water splashes, woodland ravines and every type of obstruction on the way to these premises, and I could cope with all sorts of gate, bulls, pigs and abandoned farm machinery. But almost without exception, my admission was friendly and courteous. At every place, I could expect a cup of tea or coffee with a slice of fruit cake, and in most cases something seasonally stronger, like whisky or brandy if warranted by the occasion.

Many of the farmers expected more from me – they expected me to sit down and eat their huge dinners, called lunch in less civilised areas. These are invariably massive, the logic being that the working man's body is in need of powerful fuel to keep it going correctly. The bigger the man, and the heavier his workload, the more fuel he needs to sustain him during a long working day. This logic seems eminently reasonable, because most of the farmers were huge, muscular men who kept working without a rest from dawn until dusk, their only sustenance being repeated doses of massive meals. As one farmer explained, 'Thoo needs mair petrol for bigger, faster cars than for little cars, and they go better an' all. Ma lads is all like big cars, so Ah need ti feed 'em well.'

It appeared to be the custom to offer a seat at the table to any stranger who chanced to arrive at meal time. Inevitably, there was enough food to cater for an army of unexpected visitors, and the meals were never made from fancy food. It was all good plain Yorkshire grub, substantial and tasty, comprising local dishes like potato and onion pie, or roast beef and Yorkshire pudding, or joint of lamb with roast potatoes. Homemade soup was invariably offered, with sweets like steamed treacle puddings, apple pie and custard, or fruit pies of most kinds. Rice pudding was common, as was any milk pudding, and a cup of tea concluded the meal, with buns, ginger bread or fruit cake. These were everyday meals, not feasts for special occasions.

This typical farm dinner (lunch) was followed by a light tea around five o'clock which was something like a fry-up of sausages, black puddings, potato, bacon, eggs and tomatoes, with a light sweet like tinned fruit and a cup of tea with buns, cakes or biscuits. Supper was similar …

Because the farmers of the moors ate so well and so bounteously, they beamed with health and the hard slog of their daily toil never appeared to have any ill effects. The volume of their unceasing toil would shame today's so-called workers, and their appetites would make a Roman feast look like a Sunday School tea party.

After a few months of patrolling and visiting my friends on the moors, I learned never to pack myself a meal. I also learned not to return home for my refreshment breaks. I ate with whomever I called upon around midday or at any meal time and it was deemed discourteous to refuse this hospitality. Thus I had many superb eating houses on my daily rounds, and my moorland patrolling became a gastronomic delight.

This applied equally to other routine callers, like the postman, the vet, the electricity meter reader and similar officials. It was during this merry round of epicurean duty that I became aware of another regular visitor to my farms.

Sometimes, the fellow was leaving as I arrived and we would hold gates open for one another; sometimes he followed me in and we would eat at the same table with eight or nine farm workers, but no one bothered with introductions. I began to wonder who he was. He appeared to visit the farms with the same frequency as myself, and always availed himself of the mountainous meals.

He used a small grey Austin A35 car, immaculately kept with its chromium shining and its coachwork polished in spite of frequent muddy excursions. He was a smart man in his forties with neat black hair, who was invariably pleasant and courteous. We passed the time of day many times, without progressing beyond that basic formality.

Inevitably, we would meet one day with sufficient time for an introductory chat and this happened one spring morning shortly before twelve noon. I arrived at Howe End Farm near Langbeck after a tortuous ride up a stone-ridden incline, and my mission was to check the particulars of Farmer John Tweddle's firearm certificate, which was due for renewal. As I parked my motorcycle against a pigsty wall, the little grey Austin chugged into the farm yard and came to a halt at my side. The neat man with black hair climbed out, clutching a briefcase in his hand.

'Morning,' I smiled, removing my crash helmet. 'You've survived the bumps, then?'

He laughed. 'Aye,' he said. 'I've grumbled at old John about his road, but he never does anything about it. He reckons if folks really want to visit him, they won't mind a few bumps and buried rocks, and if they don't want to come, they deserve to suffer a bit.'

'I'm PC Rhea,' I introduced myself. 'I'm the new policeman over at Aidensfield.'

'This is a bit off your beat, isn't it?' He closed his car door.

'Not now,' I said. 'Since they issued us with motorbikes, they've closed some beats and extended the boundaries of others. I cover a large patch now, including this end of the moor.'

'And me,' he said, offering me his hand. 'Norman Taylor, insurance man.'

We shook hands warmly.

'I've noticed you coming and going, and having those massive meals,' I laughed. 'It seems all and sundry can just stop and eat with them.'

'They're offended if you go away unfed at dinner time. It's as natural to these folks to feed their visitors as it is for, say, a policeman to give advice to a lost motorist. I think it stems from the days when visitors took days rather than hours to reach these remote places. If anyone came, they'd need feeding before they left, and I reckon these folks are continuing that custom. They haven't realised that our cars and bikes get us from place to place within minutes rather than hours.'

Together, Norman and I walked to the back door which was standing open and he entered without knocking. He walked straight to a teapot on the mantelpiece, lifted the lid and took out a £1 note. He made an entry in a book which lay beside the teapot and smiled at me.

'Monthly insurance premium,' he said. 'She always leaves it here.'

'They're trusting folk,' I commented.

'They are; they trust those who call, as if they were their own family. Mrs Tweddle is a good payer, she never forgets to leave her £1 for me once a month.'

'I'm looking for John, his firearm certificate's due for renewal.'

Norman looked at his watch. It was twelve o'clock, and he said, 'He comes in for his dinner at quarter past twelve. Elsie will be here soon – there'll be a potato and onion pie warming in the Aga.'

And he sat down.

I pondered over my next action; I ought to go into the buildings to seek my customer and Norman recognised my hesitation.

'Sit down,' he advised me. 'They'll be in soon, and it'll save you chasing about the place.'

I settled in one of the Windsor chairs and he occupied the other. We talked about our respective jobs, and it transpired he lived at Milthorpe, a hamlet on the northern edge of my beat. His agency embraced the whole of the North Yorkshire moors, a huge slice of countryside with scant population, and he told me how he enjoyed every minute of his work.

As we talked, a large rosy-cheeked woman entered the kitchen.

'Hello, Elsie,' greeted Norman.

'Hello, Norman. Nice morning,' she smiled happily. 'By, Ah've just been down hedging in our five acre. Ah'm famished – have you checked the pie?'

'No, PC Rhea came and we've been talking.'

'Oh,' she said, looking at me. 'Thoo'll be after our John?'

'Firearm certificate,' I told her. 'It's due for renewal.'

'He'll be in soon,' and she went about her business of examining the pie in the Aga. A delicious smell wafted into the kitchen as she opened the door and examined her handiwork. There were no introductions, no fuss over me, no false niceties. I was here, and that was it.

She lifted the steaming pie from the oven and prodded the thick, brown crust with her finger. It was contained in a huge brown earthenware dish and there was enough for a table of eight or nine people. She placed it on the Aga to keep warm and laid the table. She set four places, I noted, four knives, four forks and four spoons. No table cloth and no condiments. There was a good deal of pleasant small-talk between herself and the insurance man, and then big John entered. He saw me and Norman, nodded briefly and went to the sink where he washed his hands thoroughly with a grease-removing agent, then swilled his face with cold water.

'Bin greasing machinery,' he informed us. 'Spring time comes fast, eh? Winter's gone and next thing we know, it's time to get cracking, and my awd tackle allus gits rusted up.'

Having washed, he plonked himself in a chair at the table and his wife pulled a hot dinner plate from her Aga and filled it with a massive helping of steaming potato and onion pie. The crust must have been an inch thick, and the pie filling consisted of sliced potato, onions and gravy, masses of it. The pie had no bottom or sides – just the rich food with a heavy lid of luscious pastry.

'Norman,' and she filled a plate for him, and then looked at me. 'Sit there, Mr Rhea,' and she pointed to the fourth chair. It was not a request and not really an invitation. Because I was here, it was understood I would eat.

I was not used to this hospitality and my face must have registered surprise. Even though I knew of this custom, its manner of execution was strange to me.

'Come on, Mr Rhea,' said John munching at the crust. 'There's no time to waste.'

And so I found myself tackling a gorgeous pie. It needed no flavouring with salt or pepper, but there was far too much. I daren't leave any, and was on the point of finishing the first helping when she ladled a second dollop on to our plates. How Norman coped I do not know, but I must admit I struggled. Eventually, I cleaned it all away. I saw Norman and the others cleaning up the gravy with a lump of pie crust held in their fingers. Luckily I had some left, so I copied them.

The result was four very clean plates.

Mrs Tweddle took our plates and placed them on the Aga; then she lifted an equally large glass dish of rice pudding from the oven. It had a tough brown skin on top, and the contents beneath were creamy and thick. She spooned generous helpings on to our first course plates and I now knew why we'd cleaned them so thoroughly. I must admit I was surprised at this but I later learned it is a widely practised custom on moorland farms. And it saves washing up!

After the final cup of tea with cakes and biscuits, Norman bade farewell and I was left with John. He produced a whisky bottle because it was our first meeting, and over a strong draught we completed his application form for renewal of his certificate. I collected the half-crown fee and left the farm, having made new friends.

As things often tend to work out, I bumped into Norman many times during my farm visits. His little grey car would be negotiating tricky farm tracks and moorland roads as he went about collecting his premiums and offering advice to his many customers. I learned that his honesty was such that everyone left their doors open, from big farms and houses to tiny cottages and bungalows, and he knew where each person left his premiums. I never knew the name of his company because everyone called it Norman's Insurance, and this is how I came to refer to it. The money left on tables or doorsteps was always for Norman's Insurance.

But his activities began to interest me. He appeared to be something of a general dealer because I often saw him carrying rolls of wire netting, hunting boots, old pictures or other objects to his car. On one occasion he carried a brace of pheasants, and on others I saw him variously with a three-legged stool, a brace and bit, a clip rug, two hunting prints, a car tyre, some brass lamp holders from an ocean-going liner, a garden bench, a scythe, a butcher's bike, a side of ham and a Victorian fire screen.

During the times we passed or met one another, he never enlightened me about his extra-insurance activities, and I did not ask. One does not pry too deeply because it indicates a betrayal of trust, but I did consider asking around to discover what he was up to. But, in the event, that course of action became unnecessary.

By chance, I was called urgently to Norman's village of Milthorpe because a visitor had reported his jacket and wallet stolen. It seems he had removed them while changing the wheel of his sports car, and when he'd finished the job, his sports jacket, and the wallet it contained, had vanished. I was on patrol at the time, astride my Francis Barnett, and the radio summoned me to the scene of this foul crime.

It took me thirty-five minutes to arrive, and I found the irate motorist waiting near his Triumph Spitfire. I eased to a halt, parked the motorbike and removed my crash helmet. I left it on the pillion.

'PC Rhea,' I introduced myself. 'Are you the gentleman who has lost a jacket?'

'Not lost, Constable. Stolen,' affirmed the man. He was tall and well-spoken with expensive clothes which spoke of a nice line in tailoring. His hair was plastered across his scalp with some kind of hair cream and he seemed totally lacking in humour. On reflection, it's not funny having your belongings stolen while changing a car wheel.

'Tell me about it,' I took out my pocket book. He told me he was Simon Christie from Southwark, having a touring holiday alone in the moors. His wallet contained some sixty pounds in notes, together with his driving licence and other personal papers. The jacket, he explained, was of Harris tweed, tailor-made in London and worth a lot of money. I didn't doubt it.

I asked how on earth he'd managed to get it stolen.

'That is something you are here to establish,' he said haughtily. 'Look, I got a puncture in my front offside tyre, and stopped right here to change wheels. I removed my jacket and placed it on the railings at the rear of the car. I worked on the wheel at the front, and when I'd finished, my jacket was gone.'

'How long did it take to change the wheel?' I asked.

'Ten minutes, maybe less,' he said.

'And did anyone walk past while you were working?'

He shook his head. 'I'd swear that no one came past, Constable. I'd swear it.'

'Are you sure it's gone? It's not in your boot, is it?'

He sighed the sigh of a man who'd hunted everywhere, but raised the boot lid. No jacket. I looked in the car, under the car, over the hedge and everywhere. It had vanished.

'I'll make enquiries in Milthorpe,' I promised. 'Can I contact you locally if I find it?'

'You sound hopeful, Constable?' There was almost a smirk in his voice.

'This is a very small community, Mr Christie,' I said in reply. 'If anyone has stolen your jacket, someone here will have seen the culprit. These folks have eyes everywhere.'

I made a deliberate attempt to sound confident, for I

imagined his coat had been lifted from the verge by a passing tramp or hiker. If so, the locals would know where he was. I had complete faith in my ability to recover this property and emphasised that point.

'I'm staying at the Crown Hotel in Ashfordly,' he said. 'I'll be there for a further four nights, Constable.'

'I'll be in touch before you leave,' I assured him.

Having obtained a detailed description of his jacket and of his wallet, I watched him leave with a roar of his throaty exhaust, and set about detecting Milthorpe's crime of the century. When beginning enquiries in any village, it is prudent to begin at the Post Office. Village post offices are replete with gossip and information about local people and their affairs, so I strolled into the tiny, dark shop with its multitude of scents, dominated by soap and polish.

At the sound of the door bell, a young woman appeared and smiled sweetly. She would be in her late twenties, I guessed, and had pleasing dark hair and a ready smile full of pure white teeth. She was very young to be a village post mistress, I thought.

'I'm PC Rhea,' I announced, conscious that my helmet was on the pillion of my bike some distance away, and my motorcycle suit bore no insignia. I could be anybody.

'I saw you arrive,' she said, as if to confirm my belief in the all-seeing eyes of village people. 'You were talking to that man with the sports car.'

'He's had his jacket stolen,' I informed her. 'It's odd – it was taken during the few minutes he was changing his wheel.'

'That'll be Arthur,' she said immediately. 'He's always stealing – he once stole a pair of slippers I'd left outside, and he takes anything – trowels, flower pots.

We daren't leave anything lying about.'

'Oh, I see,' I now had a name. Just like that. I hate to admit I didn't know Arthur, but I had to ask where he lived.

'Where's he live?' I asked.

She pointed out of the window. 'Of course, you're new,' she smiled again. 'You won't know him. He's at Heather Cottage, next door to Mr Taylor, the insurance man.'

Until now, I had forgotten that this village was the home of Norman the insurance man, and was pleased to be reminded of the fact. I followed the line of her pointing finger and saw a neat cottage built of mellow brick. It had bow windows at the front and a red pantile roof, typical of the area. Next door was a larger house standing in its own grounds, and she confirmed that the latter belonged to Norman.

I left the little shop just in time to pause at the edge of the road for a tractor and trailer to pass. Behind I noticed Norman's little grey car and waved an acknowledgement. He saw me, and the procession pulled up at his house. He got out and shouted, 'Hello, Mr Rhea, good to see you.'

'And you, Norman,' I walked across to him.

'What's this then?' he asked. 'Business?'

'Yes,' I said. 'A theft.'

'Here in Milthorpe?' he asked, eyebrows rising.

'A motorist stopped to change a wheel,' I explained, 'and took his jacket off to work upon it. Someone stole it as he worked.'

'That'll be Arthur, next door,' beamed Norman. 'You'll find the jacket there, I'm sure.'

'Yes, the girl at the Post Office said so.'

'Come in for a cup of coffee when you've got the

jacket back,' he invited. 'I'm just taking delivery of some bantams.'

I glanced at the tractor and trailer, and noticed a farm lad standing beside the trailer, awaiting Norman's instructions. On the trailer stood a large wire-netting cage containing a dozen white bantams.

Recalling his other acquisitions, I said, 'You're a bit of a dealer, are you?'

'It's more of a bartering system,' he told me. 'These are insurance premiums. This lad's father is hard up at the moment, so I've accepted these bantams as his monthly payment.'

'It seems a good system!' I laughed.

'I've got all sorts,' he said. 'Look, you go and find Arthur, and then come in. By then, we'll have this crate of bantams off and my good lady will brew us a cuppa. I'll show you round my garden, and you can see some of my better insurance premiums!'

I chuckled at the notion, and opened the gate of Heather House. At the sound of the sneck, an aged black and white cur dog ambled from the rear of the cottage and wagged his tail in greeting. I patted him and approached the front door, the dog following closely with his old grey muzzle nudging my legs and his tail lashing backwards and forwards in happy greeting.

I knocked and waited. Soon, a grey-haired man with a big white moustache and rosy cheeks opened the door.

'Yes?' he demanded.

'PC Rhea,' I said. 'I'm the new policeman at Aidensfield.'

'Oh,' he said. 'And Ah'm Dawson. Edgar Dawson.'

So this wasn't Arthur. I wondered if Arthur was the

fellow's son, perhaps someone who was a bit simple. The dog fussed about as we talked, and I patted his head, an action which caused the tail to wag even more furiously.

'I've come about Arthur,' I said.

'What's he pinched now?' the man stood on the top step and glared at me.

This was an easy interview. 'A jacket and wallet,' I told him. 'You might have seen the sports car down the village? The driver changed a wheel and had his jacket and wallet stolen as he worked.'

'Ah'll skin him, so Ah will!' snapped the man. 'If it's not one thing, it's another. He never stops. Ah've thrashed him and belted him, but it's no good, Mr Policeman ... come with me.'

Sighing the sigh of a weary man, he led me and the dog around to the rear of the cottage, and into a shed. The shed door stood wide open and he beckoned me to follow inside. And there, lying on the floor beside a grubby rug, was the sports jacket. He picked it up and handed it to me. I looked inside the pocket – the wallet was there and when I checked inside, the cash and the driving licence were present. Nothing had been touched, and the name inside the wallet confirmed it was Simon Christie's property.

'Thanks Mr Dawson, I'm delighted. Now, I'd like to talk to Arthur about it.'

'It's not damaged, is it?' he asked me.

I examined the jacket, but other than some flecks of dust from the floor of the shed, it appeared undamaged.

'No,' I assured him, 'it's not damaged. Now where's Arthur – I'd like to talk to him.'

'He'll not understand a word thoo says, Mr Policeman.' There was a twinkle in his eye.

Suddenly, I began to feel uncomfortable. I could write off the whole affair but felt duty-bound to talk to Arthur and to ask him for an explanation. Larceny was larceny, even though the property had been recovered intact, and I was obliged to take legal proceedings. In those days, it was unlawful to conceal a felony, and larceny was classified as a felony.

'Can you take me to him please?' I asked, speaking with authority.

'He's right beside thoo, lad,' beamed Mr Dawson, and I turned to see the happy dog thrashing his tail as I caught his eye.

'You mean this is Arthur?'

'Aye, Ah thought thoo knew that. He's my dog, twelve years old he is, and a real rogue. Now if yon jacket's damaged, go and see Mr Taylor next door, and he'll settle up with t'loser.'

'Mr Taylor?'

'Aye, t'insurance man. Arthur's allus been one for pinching things so I've got him insured. He once pinched a workman's trowel and chewed t'handle to bits. He loves gardening tools. Spades, rakes, owt with a wooden handle. Clothes an' all. He'll get on his hind legs and pull clothes off t'washing lines, knickers, stockings, trousers, sheets … you name it, and Arthur's pinched it. So Ah got him insured and if there's any damage, Norman's insurance pays out.'

'Is there anything else that's stolen in here?' I asked, looking at the objects that filled the place.

'No, Ah've looked. Ah checks it reg'lar at night before Ah turns in, and if there's summat that's not mine, Ah leave it at t'Post Office. Ruth puts it on t'counter and whoever's lost it gets it back. It's only strangers that doesn't understand, Mr Policeman.'

'I'm not surprised,' I laughed, and the dog's nose nudged me. I turned to address Arthur, the thieving dog. 'Arthur, you are not obliged to say anything, but what you do say will be taken down in writing and may be given in evidence!'

The tail thumped my leg as Arthur acknowledged the official short caution, but he made no reply. I wondered what Sergeant Blaketon would make of this – I wondered about writing a full report and charging Arthur as a joke. I wondered if it would pass through our administrative system and get filed at Headquarters?

Having recovered the jacket, I returned to my motorcycle and tucked the clothing into my pannier before visiting Norman. The tractor and empty trailer was just leaving, and Norman was at the gate.

'You've seen Arthur?' he laughed.

'Nobody said he was a dog!' I grumbled. 'I could have made a right fool of myself.'

'Sorry, we all know him. Every time something is stolen in Milthorpe, we know it's Arthur. Did old Dawson tell you I've got his dog insured for causing damage?'

'He did,' I let myself through his gate. 'He sounds a real character, that dog.'

'He is! He's always chasing lady dogs too, so I had to insure him against getting bitches pregnant. He once put a pedigree bitch in the family way and there was hell on about it. So Mr Dawson has him comprehensively insured against causing damage and distress of all kinds. Only last year, I paid out twice for getting bitches into trouble – if that dog was human, he'd be doing umpteen prison stretches by now. As it is, we accept him for what he is, a likeable old rogue. His love life would cripple a lesser dog. He's incredible!'

Norman's wife, Eva, was a charming woman who produced a hot cup of strong tea and a plate of scones, and soon we were all chattering like old friends. Norman told me of his bartering system, explaining how the hill farmers upon the moors had very little cash. All their work went into real estate and property, so when they died, their families inherited a great deal, while the unfortunate farmer had worked for a pittance all his life.

Norman's system involved many deals. He told me about one farmer who did all his gardening, one who did his painting and plumbing, another who repaired his car and others who regularly donated eggs, bacon, ham, milk and potatoes as methods of payment for their insurance premiums.

After the cup of tea, he led me down the garden. The bantams were pecking happily at their new piece of earth, and a peacock stalked majestically up and down in a cage. 'From the big house,' he said confidentially. 'Times are hard all over.'

Two goats and a Siamese cat were shown to me, and a new pedal cycle graced the garage. The real gems were in a long narrow shed at the far end of the garden. He opened the doors to reveal a veritable treasure trove of objects, most of which would be ideal curios for a rural museum. The walls were hung with old advertising signs in enamel, house signs and shop signs; every kind of gardening implement and carpentry tool was there, many of them obsolete, and along the base of one wall there were stone troughs and foot scrapers set in stone. It was an Aladdin's cave of rural objects, of obsolete items which would never again grace the homes of our people and which would, but for

Norman's care, have disappeared for ever.

'All these have been collected in lieu of insurance premiums,' he told me. 'I could sell some of the things, but if anything's got historic or sentimental value of any kind, I like to keep it. I've a three-seater tandem in that shed at the bottom of the garden, and a 1927 motorcycle in full working order. I can't sell stuff like that, can I? But I do sell a lot – I've got to, to keep my books right!'

I spent a fascinating hour with him, and wondered how many rural insurance agents traded in this way.

But it was time to leave.

I thanked Norman for his interesting tour and assured him we'd meet again. I invited him and Eva to pop into my hilltop house any time, and off I went.

While driving through Brantsford on the way home, I noticed Mr Christie's sports car parked outside a small café and decided I should reveal to him the results of my enquiries. I pulled up and parked the motorcycle on its stand before entering the café. I left the jacket in my pannier for the moment, just in case he was not in here.

But he was drinking a cup of tea and as he recognised me, his eyebrows rose sharply.

'Ah, Constable! And have you detected the crime of the century?'

I smiled diffidently at him.

'Yes,' I said. 'I saw your car and thought I'd mention it. I have your jacket and your wallet – and the cash. It's all there.'

He drained the tea and said, 'No, really?'

'I'll fetch it in for you.'

'No, I'm leaving. I've paid, by the way,' and he followed me outside where I unstrapped my pannier and lifted out his precious belongings. He readily identified them as his property and checked the contents of his wallet at my request. Nothing was missing, and I then asked him to check everything for damage. There was none.

'Constable, this is marvellous. You've traced the thief too, I take it?'

'Yes, and I have cautioned him about his future conduct!' I smiled.

'You'll be proceeding to court though?' he queried.

'Not on this occasion,' I told him with all seriousness. 'The matter has been dealt with and my enquiries are over.'

'But Constable, I am a solicitor, and I know that it is an offence to conceal a felony …'

'There was no felony, Mr Christie,' I interrupted him.

'There was a theft …' he began.

'It was no felony,' I continued.

'Who took my jacket?' he demanded. 'Are you covering up for a local thief or something? This is serious.'

'His name is Arthur,' I said, 'and he is a twelve-year-old cur dog.'

Christie paused as if not believing my words.

'A dog?' he grinned suddenly, not sure whether I was joking.

'A dog.' I told him about the insurance scheme which catered for Arthur's incurable kleptomania.

He laughed loudly in the middle of the street, and slung his jacket over his shoulders. 'Well done, Constable, well done. Yes, I like it – a nice one. A dog, eh? Called Arthur?'

'Yes, Mr Christie.'

'I don't believe you!' he chuckled. 'But I like your

style. Wait until I tell them in London about this.'

And off he strode towards his waiting car. I watched him drive away in a flurry of exhaust fumes and wondered what he would tell his sophisticated colleagues about law enforcement in rural North Yorkshire.

Chapter 4

'There are two classes of pedestrians in these days of
reckless motor traffic – the quick and the dead.'

LORD DEWAR

IN MY EXTREME YOUTH, lady drivers were a rarity and
when one witnessed a member of that fairest of sexes
driving a motor-car, the sight was enough to make one
stand and stare, before broadcasting the sighting to
one's friends. Ladies as passengers were not
uncommon, but it is fair to say that the skill of guiding
a moving motor vehicle from place to place was usually
entrusted only to the male of the human species.

Gradually, however, the ladies began to assume the
mantle of masculinity and independence, and in
addition to smoking or wearing slacks instead of skirts,
they took lessons in the art of driving motor-cars. It
wasn't long before ladies were driving all sorts of
vehicles but I cannot recall my first sight of a lady
behind the wheel. It cannot have been that unusual or
important.

Certainly, this form of emancipation occurred long
before I joined the Police Force, consequently by the
time I had passed through training school, ladies were
frequently seen at the wheel. We were taught
diplomacy when asking their age, and admittedly, there
were jokes or tales about their driving. One instructor

told us how he'd stopped a lady motorist in Middlesbrough for driving at 40 miles an hour in a built-up area, to which she retorted, 'Don't be ridiculous, I haven't been driving for an hour, and I certainly haven't done forty miles.'

There were those who hung their handbags on the chokes and wondered why the car engine throbbed and smoked; there were those who pointed at scenic things through open windows and confounded those driving behind into thinking all manner of things which were far from the truth, and there were those who depended upon a man to keep the machine roadworthy after their exertions.

It must be said that there were many ladies who coped admirably with the motor-car and its moods. One lady who thought she fitted into this category was Esme Brittain, a lovely looking woman in her late forties who drove a white Morris Minor. She was blessed with a pneumatic figure, jet black hair and lovely white teeth, all enhanced by dark eyes and gorgeous legs. She had been married but the outcome of that association was something of a mystery because the male half had vanished long ago, leaving Esme with her little cottage and a Yorkshire Terrier. There were no children of the union, and Esme earned her living by teaching pottery and selling her distinctive products to tourists and craft shops.

Esme was a charmer. Of that there was no doubt, and many a hunting male had attempted to change her tyres, check her batteries and clean her plugs but she politely and firmly rejected and resisted all approaches, however oblique. Although she never said so, the villagers felt she'd been let down by her erring husband to such an extent that she trusted no man. It must be

81

said, however, that she never criticised her missing husband, nor did she grumble about his absence. She lived as if he'd never existed and perhaps she had the ability to blot him from her life and memory. I shall never know, but she certainly kept all men at a respectful distance, particularly from her emotions.

Nice as she was, and beautiful as she looked, Esme in a car was a threat to society. She reduced the most innocent of motor-cars to the status of a guided missile, and floated through heavy traffic as if she were a balloon which would bounce off obstructions. How she avoided accidents was never known, because her driving ability was appalling in the extreme. She had no idea of road sense, car care or any of the niceties of motoring. She just climbed in and set off, heedless of other road users. Yet she survived.

Such was her reputation that the local people kept well out of her way. The moment Esme was mobile, everyone kept off the streets until her little Morris Minor was safely beyond the outskirts of Maddleskirk. What happened beyond those boundaries was none of their business, and they had the sense not to find out.

The trouble was that Esme's adventures frequently became my business. Her erratic excursions invariably had a startling conclusion, and if she entered any of the conurbations within striking distance of the village she could be guaranteed to collect a summons for obstructing the highway, illegal parking, lack of proper lights, careless driving or some other trifling traffic infringement. Esme's trouble was that she never reported to the local police as advised in the tickets which were plastered about her windscreen after such indiscretions, consequently when the distant police traced her through the registration number, I was given

82

the task of interviewing her for her regular and multifarious misdeeds. In this way, I became acquainted with the lovely Esme.

She constantly and charmingly admitted her errors and got fined by many magistrates, yet her adventures never made any obvious impression upon her. She never altered her ways or improved her driving, and yet she was never involved in a serious accident. I considered that to be miraculous.

It is not to say, however, that she was not a danger, because she did occasionally cause people to jump off their pedal cycles or motorists to abandon the road in order to preserve their own lives or safeguard their vehicles. But she avoided most collisions.

One exception involved three visiting ladies from a Women's Institute in County Durham. One lovely Sunday morning in late April, a bus load of them had travelled from the pit villages up north, and had ventured south to North Yorkshire in order to visit Rannockdale and its acres of wild bluebells. *En route*, the coach had stopped at a remote moorland hamlet called Gelderslack so that the ladies could form a queue at the toilet and buy coffee at a local café. The driver told them the break would be for three quarters of an hour, because he'd calculated it was the shortest time that a bus load of chattering women could each visit a single toilet. Such is the wisdom of bus drivers.

The first three ladies in the loo queue, having achieved their purpose, were also first in the coffee queue and therefore first out of the tiny village café. To while away the time until the last of their kin had taken on coffee and poured off water, they settled on a seat in the village. The seat in question had been presented to Rannockdale by Sir Cholmely Brown, and it occupied a prime site at the eastern side where it overlooked Surprise View. The place was visited by tourists, cameramen and Americans, all of whom admired the stupendous views from this summit. The three satisfied ladies managed to occupy that hallowed place for a few blissful minutes; for them, it represented rural solitude, because here they could sit and admire the view while their friends queued.

But they had reckoned without Esme and her doubtful driving ability. Through one of those awkward coincidences, Esme arrived in Gelderslack at the same time as that bus, because she was thinking of trading her little Morris Minor in part exchange for a large Humber Snipe. Gelderslack garage had a gleaming black Humber for sale, and so Esme arrived that day to inspect and test it. The benevolent garage proprietor, on seeing the immaculately polished Morris, readily consented to Esme taking the Humber for a test run. She climbed into the driving seat, coped with the starter and the gears, and drove the huge car into the spring sunshine.

All went well until she reached Surprise View. At that point, she recalled that she was not very good at descending steep hills, so decided to turn around and go the other way. To achieve this about-turn, it was necessary to execute a three-point turn and Esme succeeded in guiding the front wheels of the Humber into the side of the road as the prelude to her change of direction. This meant that the nose of the Humber was a very few inches from the back of the seat upon which sat the three unsuspecting ladies from the County Durham W.I. In their state of happiness, they failed to register any alarm at the proximity of Esme and the big car.

She stopped without any trouble, placed the gears in reverse and let in her clutch. Sadly, she'd erroneously engaged a forward gear and the huge car nudged forward and touched the rear of the seat. Esme halted its forward rush, but it succeeded in tipping the seat forward and toppling the three ladies into an untidy and ungainly heap on the ground overlooking Surprise View. Highly apologetic, Esme rushed to their aid, returned the seat to its correct position, and dusted down the surprised trio. Rather baffled by this turn of events, they re-settled on their seat and gazed airily across the moor.

Her apologies accepted, Esme resumed her position in the driving seat and had another crack at selecting reverse. As she let in the clutch for the second time, the car misbehaved yet again and leapt forward to tip up the seat. Once again, the three surprised ladies slid off and crumpled into a pitiful heap with the seat resting on top of them. Esme blushed furiously. She rushed out of the Humber and re-positioned the seat yet again, dusting them down with her hands and expressing her most profuse apologies. She tried to explain about the gears, but they glared at her angrily; gone was their northern *bonhomie* as they sat heavily upon their precious seat, furious at the indignities they had suffered. One had even laddered her stockings.

Very nervously, Esme re-entered the waiting Humber and with extreme care, selected reverse. Most gingerly, she let in the clutch but this car was enjoying itself. It moved forward for the third time, and before she could halt its short progress, it once again touched the back of the seat and tipped it forward. For the third time, the W.I. ladies slid to the ground, a miserable, angry heap of feminine wrath. Now, they could endure no more and chased Esme from the Humber. She managed to reach sanctuary in the garage and sought protection from the man who'd loaned her the wilful vehicle.

But luck was on Esme's side because the loo queue was dwindling rapidly and the bus driver, who had witnessed the whole affair, had a sense of humour. He tooted his horn and drew his passengers back to the coach, but this did not prevent the aggrieved three from making a complaint. A day or two later, I had to interview Esme about it. Although I submitted an official report against her for careless driving, the Superintendent authorised 'No action', his reasons being, I suspect, that any magistrates listening to this complaint would dissolve into laughter and that would be undignified in a court of law.

Happily, my regular official visits to Esme did not sour our relationship. She continued to regard me as a friendly caller and never once complained about the frequency of my visits, nor did she grumble about the regular fines she attracted. She probably thought all motorists suffered in this way.

I must admit I liked her. I remember one terrible winter morning when five or six inches of snow had fallen overnight. The roads were treacherous and the small amount of traffic had compressed the snow into a sheet of dangerous ice. Maddleskirk village was blocked at both exits, for there are steep hills climbing out at each end of the village street. The early morning traffic which comprised lorries, bread trucks, tankers, post office vans and commuters' cars had all come to a standstill because each hill was impassable. I arrived on foot to have a look, and borrowed a shovel from a farmer who lived on the main street. With the shovel over my shoulder, I trudged through the blizzard conditions, intending to spread gravel across the glistening surface, and get the queue of traffic moving.

As I walked to the base of the western hill, I heard a car engine behind and turned to see Esme in her immaculate white Morris Minor. She halted at my side and wound down her window.

'Good morning, Mr Rhea,' she breezed, her lovely face wreathed in smiles and framed in a fur bonnet.

'Hello, Esme,' I greeted her. 'You're not going out today, I hope!'

'I must get to Leeds,' she said. 'I have an appointment at a craft shop this morning and can't let them down.'

'You'll never get through,' I pointed to the queue of patient drivers, all sitting at their wheels or helping to spread gravel.

'Oh, I don't worry about snow,' she said. 'I pretend I'm on a motor rally and it gets me through every time,' and with that she set her wheels in motion. Two lorry drivers who'd overheard this remark launched into a polite cheer as the gallant little Morris approached the base of the steep hill. No one had climbed it that morning; it was like glass and the skid marks etched wildly across its surface bore testimony to their efforts.

We all watched and wondered how long it was going to take to dig her out, but the little white car chugged forward and started to climb. Everyone watched in sheer amazement as Esme's car stolidly climbed that treacherous incline and vanished over the top. Others tried, but all failed.

To this day, I do not know how she achieved that, but it dawned on me that I'd never seen Esme stuck in the winter. Faith must be a wonderful thing.

I began to think Esme was invincible. Somehow, she

blazed a trail through life in her little Morris Minor and never seemed to ask help from anyone. Then, one fine morning in May, she called at my office in Aidensfield. She rang the bell, and I answered, very surprised to find her there.

'Come in, Esme,' I opened the door and she strode in. 'You've come to produce your licence and insurance again?'

'No,' she smiled. 'No, I'm not in trouble, Mr Rhea. I *can* drive without getting fined, you know. I'm not one of those silly women drivers who are always in trouble.'

'Of course not,' I pulled out a chair for her. 'Well, what's wrong?'

'I am going down to Stratford-on-Avon,' she said. 'I'm taking a friend and we are going to see some of the Shakespearian productions at the Stratford Theatre.'

'You'll enjoy it,' I smiled, for I'd seen several of their skilled interpretations of the Bard's works.

'I do have a problem,' she lowered her voice. 'I need directions to Stratford, I cannot work out my own route.'

'That should be no trouble,' I pulled a road atlas from the bookshelf in my office. 'I went a couple of years ago, and know the route well.'

'Oh, I know the route,' she said, pausing for effect.

'You do?'

'You've not heard of my problem?' she asked me solemnly.

'No.' I wondered which problem she meant. 'What problem?'

'I'm surprised no one has mentioned it to you,' she continued to talk in a low voice. 'And I'm surprised you have not noticed for yourself, Mr Rhea. I thought policemen were supposed to be very observant ...'

'I haven't been here long,' I began to make an excuse.

'My driving,' she said. 'It's the way I drive.'

'Oh, yes.' I thought of all the catastrophes she might create between Aidensfield and Stratford, and wondered if I should warn all constabularies *en route*.

She laughed and appeared able to read my thoughts, for she said, 'It's not my parking problems, Mr Rhea, or my reversing difficulties.'

'No?' I could not think of anything else right now.

'It's my inability to turn right,' she said, pausing for the awesome implications of that remark to sink into my skull.

'Turn right?' I questioned.

'Yes, I cannot turn right off a road. I go everywhere by making left turns,' she told me in all seriousness. 'I can cope with right turns off one-way streets, but not on ordinary roads. Surely you've seen me coming home different ways?'

'I had no idea that was the reason,' I said. 'So you are telling me you intend to drive to Stratford-on-Avon without ever turning right?'

'Yes, that's why I came to see you. Last year, I set off to go to Harrogate to the theatre and things went fine until I came to a new one-way street in Ripon. I got hopelessly lost ...'

'What happened?' I asked, suppressing a chuckle.

'I got to Middlesbrough, miles from where I intended, and had to get a train back. It's all very embarrassing, Mr Rhea, and I cannot help it.'

'I don't know whether I'm capable of producing a route for you all that way, Esme; I wonder if there are other people like you?'

'A cousin of mine could never go around a roundabout,' she said. 'He always took the right-hand route instead of the left and got into no end of bother from the police. He blocked the whole of Newcastle upon Tyne one Saturday morning because he hit a bus on a roundabout. He was fine if he drove on the continent.'

I did not want to let her down and promised I'd do my best to find a route to Stratford-on-Avon, a distance of some two hundred miles, without her having to turn right. She was going in a fortnight's time, she told me, so there was no great rush.

With Mary's help, I settled down to work out a route and it was not as difficult as I had anticipated. Working along the main roads, I could plan the basic route bearing in mind one must make huge circular tours from time to time, and that the exits from motorways are all to the left anyway. The tricky bits were the towns, especially Stratford itself on the final lap, although I did suggest she parked on the outskirts and caught a bus into the town centre.

I calculated the length of this circuitous journey and felt she would travel at least twice the true distance, but on the appointed day she sallied forth full of confidence with a grey-haired lady passenger beaming hopefully from the front seat.

She allowed herself two days to reach her destination, and I was somewhat surprised when she rang me from Penrith in Cumberland, and then from Chester, to find out where she'd gone wrong. But she arrived safely three days later, having covered nearly eight hundred miles in large circular routes.

My plan hadn't helped because she'd missed several turnings and I'd not counted a new one-way system in Leeds. I couldn't remember including Leeds in my route, but did not argue.

I did wonder how she'd get back.

She returned a fortnight later and in the following days, I received twenty-five requests from police forces to visit her and report her for parking infringements, one-way street offences and careless driving on that trip, and they included places as far apart as Lancaster, Lincoln, Huntingdon, Warwick, Chippenham and Gateshead. But her Morris Minor hadn't a scratch, and neither had she.

In communities as small as Aidensfield, Maddleskirk and the like, there is usually one eccentric motorist whose deeds are widely known to the local people, and they contrive to keep well out of the way when the said eccentric is in motion. But these villages had Esme and another. Two of them in such a small area seemed destined to bring chaos.

Cedric Gladstone was the other's name, and he lived in a nice bungalow on the edge of Aidensfield with his lovely wife and two spaniels. Cedric was a retired motor engineer, a short, tubby gent with rimless spectacles and a bristling white moustache who had, in his working life, been something of an expert at his craft. In his retirement, he spent a lot of time in his workshop, making objects which no other craftsmen would tackle due to the time and patience needed. He fashioned objects like keys for grandfather clocks or winding handles for gramophones, small tools for specialist tasks and knick-knacks for household use. He did this for fun, although he was not averse to accepting gratuities in the shape of bottles of whisky as payment for his craftsmanship.

Cedric ran an old Rover car, a lovely 1949 model in a delicate shade of tan with darker brown mudguards, and this was his pride and joy. He had spent years with this car, having bought it new, and upon his retirement had managed to acquire a comprehensive stock of spares. By this prudent advance planning, Cedric was able to keep his car on the road when others fell by the wayside or ended their life on waste tips and scrap metal dumps.

I liked Cedric. I loved to chat with him in his workshop as he filed and soldered precious little pieces of metal together to create some implement useful for an obscure task. Even in his advancing years, a pride of creation and inventiveness remained. He showed me some of the things he'd produced – trowels, a ball-point pen, thousands of keys for hundreds of jobs, a toasting fork with a shield to protect the hand from the heat of the fire, all sorts of gadgets for working in car engines, a rack for shoelaces, a toothbrush holder and so forth. It's fair to say I spent many a happy hour watching him at work in his hessian apron and battered old flat cap.

But in that beautiful car, Cedric was a changed person. His big problem was drink, and I must admit it was a long time before I realised he was an alcoholic. I might have guessed because his home was stacked with an infinite variety of whiskies, collected over many years from the Highlands of Scotland, and drunk deeply every day by a thirsty Cedric. He was a frequent visitor to the local inns where he happily drank their whisky, or the whisky of anyone who would pay for the pleasure of seeing it vanish down Cedric's throat.

It is difficult to recall exactly when I became aware of this black side of Cedric's character. Certainly, his lovely Rover was at large most days, always immaculately polished and chugging beautifully along the lanes or through the villages as Cedric and his wife, Amelia, went about their business and pleasure. I had often seen the car during my patrols, and there was never any reason to halt it or to check the driver for illegalities. It had always been carefully driven, then one spring morning, some time after arriving at Aidensfield, my professional attention was drawn to the car.

It emerged from the drive of Cedric's house and someone was grating the gears. There was an awful noise as metal fought with metal, the gears doing their best to mesh under some intolerable handicap. I stared at the immaculate little car, wondering if it was being stolen, but saw that Cedric was driving.

I watched in considerable horror, wincing at the thought of unseen damage as the lovely vehicle emerged on to the road to groan its way into the village. As I was on foot, I was not in a position to chase him, although I did follow its path, listening to the clonking noises and the agonising screeching of the protesting gears. The din ceased somewhere along the village street.

Minutes later, I found Cedric's car. It was in the car park of the Brewers Arms, neatly parked and driverless. I checked my watch – it was ten thirty, opening time. I decided to pop in to see if Cedric was ill or in need of help and found him perched on a bar stool chatting amiably with Sid, the resident barman. He looked very content and relaxed, and in his hand was a double Scotch.

'Ah, Mr Rhea, can I tempt you?' he held the glass high, his grey eyes glistening with evident pleasure as he scrutinised the bronze contents.

'No, thank you, Cedric, not when I'm on duty.' I couldn't face a whisky or any alcohol at this time of morning.

'I'm having a coffee, Mr Rhea,' Sid offered.

'There's some in the pot.'

'I'd love one, Sid,' and with no more ado, he produced a coffee pot and poured a steaming mugful. I removed my uniform cap and settled on a stool at Cedric's side. He looked in the bloom of youth now, sitting high on that stool with his back as straight as a ramrod, and his white moustache bristling with energy. His thick white hair bore no signs of thinning and his eyebrows matched his hair, thick and white, all set in a healthy pink face. His clothes were neat too, all cavalry twills, Harris tweeds and wool shirts with brogue shoes and green woollen socks.

As I talked about nothing in particular, I realised I'd often seen his car here, never thinking he was in the pub. I thought he parked it as a matter of convenience for the shop or the post office, because at home I'd never seen him drink heavily. True, he'd shown me his collection of malt whiskies, but I'd never seen evidence of alcoholism. But now, sitting at his side as he rhapsodised over the drink and recalling the method of the Rover's arrival, I realised I had a hardened drinker on my patch – and a motorist into the bargain.

This was long before the days of breathalysers and samples for laboratory analysis. In order to secure a conviction for drunken driving, it was necessary to prove beyond all doubt that the driver was under the influence of drink or drugs to such an extent as to be incapable of having proper control of the vehicle when driving or attempting to drive on a road. This was done by doctors; they were called by the police and conducted hilarious examinations of suspects by making them walk along white lines chalked upon the floor or asking them to add up sums of figures which not even the doctor could calculate correctly. The outcome was that many grossly drunken individuals managed to survive those primitive tests to escape conviction for an offence which so easily caused death to others. This was the reason for the introduction of the breath tests and the need for scientific analysis of the blood or urine to determine the alcohol level in the body. Thus, the guesswork and favouritism was eliminated.

But none of this affected Cedric. He was drinking long before such progress came to harass drunks. I looked closely at him. There was no sign of drunkenness. He was sitting unaided on a bar stool, with no back rest and he was not swaying nor was his speech slurred. He was conducting a most rational conversation with myself and Sid, and it was certainly not feasible to consider him drunk in charge of his vehicle. This differed from drunken *driving* because a person could be in charge of his van or car even when asleep in the back seat. Cedric was in charge of his car right now, sitting at that bar with the keys in his pocket...

But he was not drunk.

Once more, I recollected the pained howls from his car as it negotiated our village street and concluded something must be wrong with it.

'Is the car all right, Cedric?' I ventured to ask during a lull.

'The car? It's fine, Mr Rhea. Why do you ask?'

'I was walking up the village as you left home. It sounded as if the gears were fighting to jump out of their little box.'

'My fault,' he laughed. 'I'm not at my best first thing, you know. I'm getting like my old car, I need a few minutes to get warmed up.'

I laughed it off, but did notice Sid gave me a sideways glance. At the time, I failed to read any significance into his action, but some time later I came to realise what he was trying to tell me.

On several occasions afterwards, I saw Cedric leave the pub at closing time after lunch, each time manoeuvring his lovely Rover out of the car park with the smoothest of motions and the utmost skill. There was never a rattle or a grating of gears; his driving was perfect. No drunk could achieve that standard of driving, I told myself.

It would be four or five months later, when I was again walking in the village in civilian clothes, enjoying a day off duty. I overheard the noisy approach of a car. The din was terrible; gears grated, brakes screeched, tyres fought with the road and sometimes the horn blared. I turned to find Cedric's immaculate car bearing down on me. I stood aghast, watching the lovely old car struggle along the main street, and then it turned into the pub car park. I watched.

Cedric climbed out. Or rather, he staggered out. He ambled haphazardly across the empty park towards the front door of the Brewers Arms, and vanished inside seconds after the stroke of ten thirty. I was off duty, but Cedric had been drinking …

I hurried inside, and was in time to see him struggling to mount the bar stool. Sid was helping him and in moments, Cedric was perched high on the stool beaming at a full glass of whisky on the counter. Before I could climb the few steps into the bar, he picked up the glass and drained it at a gulp.

I rushed in.

'Cedric,' I cried. 'For God's sake no more … the way you drove that car …'

'Ah, Mr Rhea,' he turned to greet me, smiling all over his rosy face with his eyes full of happiness. 'Good to see you. Have a drink – I see you're not on duty.'

'No thanks,' I declined, partly due to his state. 'I can't drink that stuff this early. Look,' I tried to talk to him. 'I've just seen you drive in here, Cedric, and you must have been drunk, the way you drove your car …'

'No,' he beamed at me benevolently. 'I've not had a drop – not until this one,' and he lifted his empty glass, and handed it to Sid for a refill.

Sid poured a generous helping and passed it back to Cedric, who tossed it down his throat with a smile.

'Nectar of the Gods,' he addressed the empty glass. 'Water of life, aqua fortis, aqua vitae, eau de vie, usquebaugh, perfume of Arabia …'

'Cedric, you must not drink and drive, it's dangerous – and illegal,' I added.

'No one has ever seen me the worse for drink when I'm driving,' he said quite coherently. 'And no one ever will, Mr Rhea, I assure you.'

'But I saw you just now, Cedric …'

'Stone cold sober, Mr Rhea. I was stone cold sober. I've told you before, it takes me a long time to get warmed up on a morning.'

Sid interrupted. 'He's right, Mr Rhea. You'll never see him worse for drink – he drinks whiskies, nothing else.' Again, I noticed the sideways glance from Sid and knew I was wasting my time. Whatever had caused Cedric to drive so awfully was not drink. Maybe he was genuinely slow at getting mobile on a morning. He must be all of seventy and it did occur to me that he might be suffering from an illness of some kind. Perhaps he was rheumaticky and needed time before his ageing limbs functioned correctly.

I left the Brewers Arms and continued along the village to do some shopping for Mary. Later that day, we placed the four children in the rear of our battered Hillman and set sail for the moors, there to enjoy the space and beauty of this fine scenery. And as I motored through Aidensfield after lunch, I saw the lovely Rover emerge from the car park of the pub. I slowed a little, and turned down my window to listen for those awful noises but it moved beautifully along with never a murmur and never a fault in its driving technique. Cedric was on his way home. He'd been in the pub since ten thirty, and it was now two thirty, with four hours of heavy drinking a distinct possibility.

I watched as the exquisite little car motored happily out of sight, and I never saw a hint of illegal motoring.

It would be four or five days later when I next called at the Brewers Arms. It was late one evening, and I was on a routine pub visit, dressed in uniform to show the presence of the law. Sid was behind the bar, dispensing his wares on behalf of the landlord. He smiled as I entered.

'There's no trouble, Mr Rhea, not tonight. We're a bit on the quiet side.'

Sid was a pleasant chap in his mid-thirties, but something of a mystery man. Always pleasant, smart and affable, he was not married and lived on the premises, where he earned a small wage for his bar tending duties and seldom left the building. He was contentment personified.

I told him about a thief who was trying to sell cheap cigarettes; we'd received information that he was attempting to get rid of stolen cigarettes by selling them to pubs and clubs, so I was warning my own landlords to be careful. Sid listened and told me the fellow had not called here; if he did, he would ring me.

As he chattered, he beckoned me to come closer.

'It's about Cedric,' he whispered confidentially.

'Is he ill?' I asked.

'Alcoholic,' Sid told me. 'He drinks pints of whisky, and often spends all lunchtime in here, when his wife is out shopping as a rule.'

'I was sure he was drunk the other morning,' I said.

'On the way here? No, Mr Rhea. He's like that *before* he gets a drink. Once he gets himself well tanked up, he's normal. With umpteen whiskies inside him, he returns to normality. Without a drink inside him, he's a liability.'

'Are you sure?'

'I'm positive, Mr Rhea. Ask about the place, ask his wife. Without his whisky, he can't do anything properly. He shakes and garbles, and is worse than useless. Honest. He rushes up here, downs a few and within minutes is back to what we'd call normal.'

'That's crazy! How could I explain that in a court of law? How could I tell a court that Cedric's sober state is a damned sight worse than others when drunk, and when he's got a skin full of whisky, he's as normal as the most sober of judges ...' I shook my head.

'We all keep out of his way when he drives here,' he said.

'Why doesn't he walk to the pub?' I asked what I thought was a sensible question.

'He'd never get here,' said Sid in all seriousness.

'But he's got loads of whisky at home, hasn't he? I've seen them – he collects bottles of all kinds, there's hundreds in his house.'

'All locked in cabinets, Mr Rhea, by his wife. I reckon she keeps him short, and she's got them locked up for emergencies – like when visitors call, and he's got to be made presentable. She'll ration him to just enough to meet the requirements of the occasion.'

'I only hope he doesn't have an accident when he's sober!' I laughed, but was assured the villagers knew his motoring movements sufficiently well to keep out of his way. I had my doubts about visitors to the place, or holiday-makers, though.

And so I became like one of the local people. I accepted Cedric for what he was. Based on the strict wording of the Road Traffic Act 1930, Section 15, he was not committing any offence when full of whisky because the wording said, 'Being under the influence of drink or a drug to such an extent as to be incapable to having proper control of the vehicle ...'

When under the influence, Cedric had full and proper control.

I could envisage a legal puzzler should he ever collide with some other person, animal or car, but he never did. In his happy state of aqua vitae, he was in perfect control of himself and his car. When sober, he was a terrible liability.

I must admit I was concerned about my pair of unusual motorists. Esme went sailing through life in her immaculate Morris, getting eternally lost and turning left at every junction or crossroads, while Cedric cruised about with his veins full of aqua vitae. Then the inevitable happened. They were both driving along the same stretch of road at the same time.

No one will ever be sure what happened, but it seems that Cedric's Rover had emerged from his gate with Cedric in a stone-cold sober state. It was shortly before his ten-thirty trip to the Brewers Arms. At that precise moment, Esme was chugging happily along in her little car, intending to visit York and its maze of one-way streets, there to collect a few parking tickets and make many left turns.

But as Cedric clanked and jerked out of his drive, Esme was horrified to see a pheasant run into the middle of the road immediately ahead of her. Had she been able to make a swift right turn, she would have missed the stupid bird, but Esme could not make a right turn. She therefore attempted to turn left.

This put her Morris right across the path of Cedric's Rover as it surged out of the drive, and he was either lucky enough or alert enough to take avoiding action. Faced with the oncoming Morris Minor, he did something to the steering wheel which put him through the hedge at the opposite side of the road, while Esme careered straight down his drive and on to his lawn.

She knocked over his sundial and sent a rustic bench into his ornamental pond, while he staggered out of his scratched car and asked if anyone had a whisky. Esme was unhurt, if shaken, and decided not to visit York that day.

My problem was whether to classify that incident as an accident within the meaning of the Road Traffic Act, but Sergeant Bairstow's advice was invaluable. It was on occasions like this that he excelled, and I was pleased I was not reporting to Sergeant Blaketon.

'A pheasant is not an animal within the meaning of the Road Traffic Act,' Sergeant Bairstow assured me, 'and besides, the damage to both cars, slight though it was, was not caused on a road. The Rover suffered minor scratches by a hedge growing on private property, and the Minor's dents were the result of colliding with a sundial in someone's garden. Take no action, Nicholas, old son. We don't want to get

101

involved in that sort of thing, do we?'

'No, Sergeant,' I agreed with some relief.

Chapter 5

'And solitude; yet not alone, while thou
Visit'st my slumbers nightly ...'
JOHN MILTON (1608–1674) *Paradise Lost*

QUITE DISTINCTLY, TWO SHOTS rang out. They echoed
through the peaceful valley as I patrolled on foot. My
mind was far from police matters as I marvelled at the
spring colouring along the length of Rannockdale, and
at first, I paid no attention. The entire countryside in
this area is riddled with gunmen shooting; they shoot
grouse during their season, pheasant and other game
during their permitted times, and vermin all year round,
consequently a couple of bangs were of no immediate
interest.

But they came again. Two very clear shots rang out,
and they came from a shotgun, not a rifle. It wasn't
until I heard a shouting match somewhere beyond my
ken that I recognised something more than a dispute
over who'd shot which animal. There were the
unmistakable sounds of vocal threats, so I increased my
pace and listened for more indications of the precise
location.

I soon found it. As I rounded a heavily wooded
corner in the higher reaches of Rannockdale, I saw a
track leading across several fields. At the distant end

was a solitary farmhouse, and running like fury along that track was a little man in a smart grey suit. He was carrying a briefcase and holding on his trilby hat as he raced towards the Ford Prefect parked at the gate. He was clearly escaping from something.

I could hear the sound of a man's angry voice emanating from the farm house, and wondered what had prompted this confrontation. I increased my pace, anxious not to place myself in the firing line, but keen to discover whether or not this was a criminal matter in which I should take a professional interest.

As I drew closer to the Ford Prefect, the little man saw me and the expression of utter relief on his face was a pleasure to behold. I was his saviour and he continued to run as if his very life depended on it, ending this gallop to freedom by clambering unceremoniously over the gate.

There he halted and leaned on his car roof as he gasped for breath. I could see that his face was pale and drawn, and sweat was flowing down his cheeks in rivulets. Clutching his chest, he stared at me with an open mouth, unable to speak of this recent horror. The words refused to come and I waited at his side, all the time conscious of the silent house across the fields. Happily, there were no further eruptions from it or its occupants.

After a good five minutes, the little man got his wind back and found he could speak.

'Officer,' he panted. 'Officer, thank God ...'

'Trouble?' I asked.

'You know that man in there?' he put to me.

I shook my head. 'Sorry,' I had to tell him. 'I'm fairly new, and I've never had to call at this house. Who lives there?'

'A lunatic called Chapman,' he said. 'Charles Alexander Chapman.'

He continued to draw in deep gasps of breath, and wiped his forehead with a coloured handkerchief after removing his trilby hat. He opened the door and placed his hat carefully on the rear seat, with his briefcase at its side.

'Inland Revenue,' he told me. 'I'm Eric Standish.'

He held out a hand for me to shake, and his grip was surprisingly strong for such a small man. I smiled and introduced myself.

'They warned me about him,' said Standish. 'It's my first visit.'

'What happened exactly?' I asked. 'I thought I heard shots back there, and shouts.'

'You did,' he confirmed. 'Shots from a twelve-bore. He was having a go at me; shooting at me!'

'I knew you chaps weren't the most popular of visitors,' I tried to cheer him up. 'You're probably more unpopular than us!'

'I accept that no one likes paying more Income Tax than necessary, but when a fellow ignores all letters and personal visits, there comes a time to call a halt. Head Office sent me to see him, to reason with him, but it's impossible, Mr Rhea. Totally impossible. He simply won't let anybody near the place.'

'You've been before – not you personally,' I corrected myself, 'but your people?'

'Regularly for years. Not one tax man has ever managed to speak to Chapman, not one. God knows how much he owes.'

'Maybe he owes nothing?' I suggested.

'He manages to live without a job,' Standish said. 'He's got investments, we're sure of it. Property too, we suspect, and we need to make an assessment of his income and his tax liability.'

'It's a very effective way of avoiding tax!' I laughed. 'Has he never paid?'

He shook his head. 'Not for years and years. He moved here from a good position with a firm in Newcastle upon Tyne twenty years ago or more, and he's lived alone ever since. Our people have tried and tried to make contact, and we fail every time.'

'I hope we don't have to visit him,' I said. 'Our uniforms might attract more target practice.'

'I'll just have to report a failure,' he spoke with a resigned air. 'I don't like reporting failures, Mr Rhea. I like to announce success in my operations.'

He entered his clean little car, started it and left me standing at the gate. I waited a few moments to see if there was any reaction and sure enough, a head appeared from an upstairs window as the car vanished along the forest road.

I could see it was a man with long grey hair and a matching grey beard, but at this distance I could not distinguish his facial features. I did see, however, that he wielded a shotgun.

'And don't you try it!' he bellowed at me, threateningly waving the gun. 'Keep off, all of you!'

And he slammed the window to withdraw into the darkness of his isolated home. I smiled to myself, marvelling at the character of a man who could keep authority at bay for so long. I wandered along my lonely route and into the tiny moorland village where my motorcycle was parked.

For me, this was an exploratory visit, my first trip to Rannockdale village in an official capacity. I was keen to learn about its people and peculiarities, so as always on such visits I had parked the motorbike to walk the streets. On this occasion my action had been rewarded by the encounter with Mr Standish, the tax man.

It was important that I learn more about the eccentric Chapman, and the ideal place to begin was the village store. I pushed open the glass-fronted door and inside, a bell rang. A middle-aged man with a white apron appeared, smiling at me as he wiped his hands on the hem.

'PC Rhea,' I introduced myself. 'I'm new here, and it's my first trip to Rannockdale. I thought I'd say 'hello'.'

'It's good of you to bother,' he finished his wiping. 'I've just been tidying some shelves at the back. Jim Freeman. My wife's called Ann, but she's out shopping for clothes, she went over to York this morning.'

'I'm at Aidensfield,' I said, removing my cap, 'but now that they've issued us with bikes, we're covering bigger patches.'

'I'm always pleased to see you chaps – fancy a coffee? I was about to have one.'

'Thanks,' and he escorted me through the shop to the living quarters where he motioned me to sit in a cosy armchair. He told me about the village, its amenities, problems, characters and gossip. I listened with interest, realising he was justifiably proud of the place and its people.

Over coffee, during which he answered the bell twice, I took the opportunity to mention Chapman and the income-tax man.

Freeman laughed loudly. 'Oh, then you've been quick to meet our prize character, Charlie Chapman, the Recluse of Rannockdale.'

'Is he really a recluse?'

'He never leaves that house – or at least, no one ever sees him leave. Rates, electricity, income tax, social services – they've all tried to get in to see him, and he gives everyone the same answer. A shotgun through the window.'

'Doesn't he ever let anyone in?' I was amazed at this. 'What's he do for food or medical supplies? Money? The essentials of life?'

'There are two people he trusts. I'm one,' he said with some pride. 'The other is Miss Stanton. She's a retired schoolteacher who lives in a cottage near the church.'

'How's he trust you? Do you get inside?'

'No, we take things up to the front door. There's a dog kennel outside the front door, and we place our things in there for him. I leave groceries once a week, and when I get there each Wednesday afternoon, he's left a note outlining the following week's requirements. I take other things for him – the mail, milk, stuff like that. I always leave them in the dog kennel with the note of the price, if any, and next time I go, the money is there, exactly right.'

'He's got a gun,' I said. 'I know a shotgun doesn't need a certificate, but has he a rifle?'

'Yes, he's got a .22 rifle which he uses for killing rooks and wood pigeons. The policeman comes once every three years to renew it. I take it up, leave the forms in the kennel and next time, I collect the filled-in forms and the money.'

At that time, a shotgun could be held without a shotgun certificate, although a gun licence was needed if the gun was taken outside the home; today, gun licences have been abolished and a shotgun requires a shotgun certificate to authorise its possession by anyone, and other firearms, except air weapons, require firearms certificates. From what I'd seen already, I knew I'd have problems with Chapman if I had ever to renew his firearms certificate. That day would surely come.

Over the following weeks, I learned that Chapman had earned his nickname 'Recluse of Rannockdale' due to his habit of writing reams of letters to people in authority. All his letters were written on beautifully printed notepaper in green typewritten characters. He claimed he was Lord Rannockdale, a cousin of the Queen, and rightful heir to several estates in the North Riding; on some letter headings, he styled himself MP, and others comprised various business letter headings, happily of fictitious firms. The recipients of his letters must have wondered who was producing such gems, but I did learn that many were aware of his activities because of constant attention by the local and national press.

It was a local newspaper which had christened him 'Recluse of Rannockdale' and the title had stuck. Every time he received wide publicity due to some idiot testing his defences for a giggle, the result was more people attempting to gain access to his house or visiting his farm with crazy notions. Some took along pressmen or cameras, for the Recluse had become something of a national celebrity. All this began some years before I arrived on the scene and in recent times, the publicity had dwindled considerably. The village people knew of his desire for the utmost privacy and respected it, and these days he lived his life almost as he wished. He was out of the nation's limelight.

That was until two burglars called.

Late one winter's evening, they decided to break

into Charlie's farmhouse. What prompted them to embark upon an enterprise of this kind, in remotest Rannockdale on a winter's evening, is still something of a mystery, but it seems they had popped into the village inn for a quick drink. They were a highly professional team of burglars from Middlesbrough and their skills had earned them a comfortable living beyond the law.

It was that same skill that almost cost them their lives. Somehow, they managed to get into Charlie's house without him realising, a feat which had defeated every caller for years. Perhaps the passage of time had helped, for there'd been no concerted attack on his home for years. We reckoned he had been lulled into a false sense of security. Be that as it may, the skilled pair had broken in and had started to rifle Charlie's precious belongings.

He had a lot of things worth stealing, like antiques, jewellery, silverware and cash, and he kept them in a bedroom. It was to that very bedroom that the hapless pair went by the light of a torch in the very early hours. They reached the room, picked the lock and entered. And there lay Charlie's treasure. They could scarcely believe their luck; it was a veritable treasure trove.

They began to place these riches into pillow cases which they used as sacks, and then Charlie approached. They heard him coming; just in time, they heard his quiet steps and saw the glint of his torch as he moved along the long corridor.

One of them, Ginger Mills, slammed the bedroom door just in time, and rammed home the lock on his side. He and his pal, Cat Christon, were locked in.

Being professionals, they appreciated this gave them time to think and plan; the householder would go downstairs to ring for the police, and while he was down there, they'd sneak out with the loot. They'd go downstairs and, if necessary, tackle him and immobilise him. So they waited; time was on their side.

Suddenly, the door panels were splintered into fragments as the twin barrels of Charlie's twelve-bore discharged themselves and his voice called, 'You can stay there, you bastards. If you climb out of the window, I'll be waiting … if you move along here, I'll be waiting …'

And as if to emphasise those words, he released a further barrage at the door. The little balls of lead shot peppered the door and blasted the interior of the room where two very alarmed burglars now crouched in fear of their lives.

He kept them there for two whole days and two whole nights, sometimes enforcing his threats with barrages of lead pellets at the shattered door. Naturally, the burglars kept out of the way, using a wall as a shield.

Then Charlie sent for the police. Early one morning, he placed a note in his kennel and this was intercepted by Mr Freeman at the shop and he rang me.

'Where are they?' I asked, surprised that Charlie's burglars had not been encouraged to leave with their backsides peppered as mementos of their visit.

'He's got them locked in the bedroom,' he told me over the telephone. 'Two, he thinks. He'll allow you to call and arrest them. He says you must be there at twelve noon today, and he'll deliver them to you at the front door.'

'Is he sure they're burglars? They're not just daft youths who got in for a dare?'

'He says burglars in his letter, Mr Rhea, and I'm

sure he's right.'

'OK,' I assured him. 'Tell Charlie I'll come with a police car.'

I rang the section office at Ashfordly and Sergeant Oscar Blaketon answered.

'Sergeant,' I said, 'It's PC Rhea. Can I use the section car today?'

'You've a motorbike, Rhea. Has it broken down or are you just feeling idle?'

'No, Sergeant,' I reasoned with him. 'It's needed to carry two burglars. I want to go up Rannockdale to arrest them.'

'Rannockdale? Who bothers to get burgled up Rannockdale?' he asked aghast. 'There's nothing up there to be burgled.'

'They're being held in a farm house,' I informed him. 'That old man who's known as the Recluse of Rannockdale has got them,' and I explained the curious circumstances.

'Oh, well, in that case you can use the car.' There was a hint of reluctance in his voice, 'but I'll come with you. It's not often we arrest burglars out here, Rhea, so you'll need support. You're coming down to the office now, are you?'

'I am, Sergeant.'

Ten minutes later, I eased my Francis Barnett into the police station yard at Ashfordly and parked it against the wall. I took my crash helmet inside and hung it on a peg, replacing it with the flat cap from my pannier.

'You drive, Rhea,' said Sergeant Blaketon, standing majestically before me in his superbly fitted uniform. He was ready to go, eager to be moving into action, but knowing him as I did, I made a careful check of the essentials. I checked the oil, water, battery and tyre pressures of the car, I made sure the lights worked, and the horn, and the windscreen wipers, and then I checked all the doors, the bonnet and the boot to ensure they closed properly. Sergeant Blaketon was a stickler for rules and routine, and I dare not omit anything. Having made a rigid check of this drill before moving out, I drove sedately across the moors in strict accordance with the driving system taught at police motoring schools.

On the way, I explained about the Recluse. I told Sergeant Blaketon how I'd learned a good deal about his lifestyle, and he listened carefully, sometimes chuckling at the antics of Charlie Chapman, and sometimes tut-tutting at Charlie's law-breaking enterprises. Blaketon had heard about him, of course; most of the local people had read of his exploits and the police, in one form or another, often caught the brunt of his anti-social behaviour.

'So what's the arrangement, Rhea? If this madman shoots everybody who puts a foot on his drive, how are we going to get the burglars out?'

'It's all arranged,' I assured him. 'We must arrive at his front door at twelve noon precisely, and he will pass them out to us.'

'Twelve noon?'

'Yes, Sergeant,' I confirmed.

'You've obviously established some sort of rapport with this character, Rhea,' and before I could tell him the truth about the note in the dog kennel, he said, 'You know, this will make the Superintendent very happy. He's been nagging about our lack of arrests, Rhea. When compared with other sections, we are not in the same league – no arrests for crime, no public order troubles or travelling thieves. But this is a good one –

two burglars at one go, Rhea. Yes. It's good, and it will improve our figures.'

It was very clear that I was in his good books, and for this I was grateful. To be on the right side of Oscar Blaketon was considered an honour, however short-lived it might be, and for a few minutes I basked in this unaccustomed glory. In his benevolence, Blaketon rambled on about the value of making arrests, of the effect they had on local villains who quaked in their shoes in anticipation of police swoops, and the need to show the public that we were, after all, a law-enforcement agency and not a charitable institution.

At one minute to midday precisely, we arrived at the entrance to the Recluse's farm. I opened the gate as Sergeant Blaketon sat stolidly in the passenger seat, then I drove through, closed the gate and climbed in beside him for the final trip. I could sense that Charlie was watching our approach, and at least he could not complain about the timing. We were accurate to the second so I had no reason to fear his shotgun.

I did realise the car was unmarked as indeed all police cars were in this region. All were a highly polished black colour with uniformed men inside, and it was this distinctive hue which identified them to the local folk. I trusted Charlie was sufficiently *au fait* with our systems to recognise our car. Happily, he did.

As we pulled up, I saw that the front door was standing wide open and two very sorry individuals in rough clothes waited just inside, with their hands on their heads. They looked awful; they looked tired, hungry and dirty as they waited in the large entrance hall of Charlie's farm. They also looked terrified because the wild and bewhiskered Charlie was standing right behind them with his shotgun at the ready.

Even as we stopped and emerged from the little car, the two men were thrust forward with the barrels of that dangerous weapon, and Blaketon said, 'Cuffs, Rhea. Handcuffs, quickly man!'

I dragged my handcuffs from my pocket – we always carried handcuffs in our left trouser pocket and the truncheon in our right – and I waited as the bearded recluse ushered them completely from his home. Sergeant Blaketon held open the driver's door and pushed the seat forward, to give them entry to the rear of the Ford. Our cars were two-door saloons for this very purpose – it was a sound idea by our Purchasing Department to buy such cars, except that it was with great difficulty that we could encourage drunks and quarrelsome folks to clamber into the confined space.

However, these two characters were in no mood for arguing. Meekly, they shuffled out of the house, prodded forward by the twin barrels of Charlie's gun. With his nose twitching in disgust at the smell that accompanied them, Sergeant Blaketon stood back as they climbed with evident relief into our rear seat.

They sat down and Charlie slammed the door of his house.

'Mr Chapman?' Sergeant Blaketon called through the closed door. 'I need to talk to you.'

No reply. Blaketon shouted several more times, but the Recluse had returned to his lair. I knew why the sergeant wished to talk to him – we needed a statement from him, a written account of the events which preceded this arrest. Without it, there was no evidence to put before a court and we might not be able to substantiate a charge of burglary, which was then a very serious crime.

'Clear off!' came the voice after Sergeant Blaketon's

repeated knocking had made his knuckles sore. 'Clear off, and take those ratbags with you.'

Sergeant Blaketon, straight as a ramrod and immaculate in his appearance, had no alternative. He turned away from the door, whirling around like a sergeant-major on parade, and made for the waiting car. I got in to the driving seat as he headed for the passenger side. The stench from our prisoners was appalling, more so in the confined space of the little vehicle.

'My God!' cried Blaketon, winding down his window. 'What's happened to you two?'

The one with short, grizzly hair answered. 'He wouldn't let us go to the toilet, Sergeant. He kept us in that bloody room without any food, heat or toilet … the man's a bloody nut-case …'

'You're nut-cases to think of burgling the old fool's house,' snapped Blaketon, holding a handkerchief to his nose. 'Anyway, you're both under arrest for burglary.'

'We can't deny this one,' the other said. 'I'm only relieved to be out of that spot, I can tell you.'

With the stinking burglars continuing to fill the car with pungent fumes, we drove through the pure countryside air with our windows wide open. To cut a long story short, they were placed in our cells and we found clean sets of clothing for them. They readily admitted housebreaking, a lesser crime than burglary, and made voluntary statements to that effect. They told how Charlie had caught them and detained them, but we got no supporting statement from him. The Detective Inspector felt the courts would accept the men's own voluntary admissions as valid evidence.

These young burglars from Middlesbrough were

each given a three-month Borstal sentence due to their age and previous record, and it was a good crime to be written off against our sectional record. For several weeks Sergeant Blaketon relived the moment of that arrest, telling all his pals and superiors about it, and there is no doubt it was the highlight of his month.

Then there came a note from Force Headquarters. It was to remind us that the firearm certificate held by Mr Charles Alexander Chapman of Rannockdale was due for renewal. It asked that an officer visit Mr Chapman to inspect the .22 firearm in question, that he supervise the completion of the relevant forms and obtain the requisite fee.

'Rhea,' said Sergeant Blaketon, 'I think the time has come for us to visit this man. I know his past record, and of his obsession with keeping people out of his premises, but this is a matter of law and we are officers of the law. I intend to visit Mr Chapman to discuss the renewal of his firearm certificate. I am sure he will look favourably upon us due to our recent part in the arrest of his burglars.'

With no more ado, Sergeant Blaketon instructed me to accompany him and we set off to enforce the law upon the impudent recluse. Sergeant Blaketon was at his bristling best, eager for the opportunity to come to terms with the eccentric man and he had the necessary forms in his briefcase. With the confidence of his kind, we could not fail. I enjoyed the trip across the forbidding moors, through avenues of pines and silver birches and across rippling streams. I had time to admire the outstanding views as we cruised into the remote valley which was the old man's home.

We pulled up at the farm gate and parked the car on the spot I'd found the Income Tax man's Ford Prefect all those weeks ago.

'You remain here, Rhea,' instructed Sergeant Blaketon. 'This is a task for a mature officer. It needs the skill of someone with deep experience and an understanding of the human mind. If two officers walk to that door, it will unnerve the fellow, so I will approach alone. I will take the renewal forms with me, and I will politely ask him to complete them as prescribed by the Firearms Act, 1937. Observe my approach, Rhea, and learn by my manner.'

'Certainly, Sergeant,' and I watched with bated breath as he tried to open the gate, but it had been tied with rope after our recent visit. He had to climb over, not the most impressive of actions by a man of his calibre, but soon he was striding manfully and majestically along the track to the distant front door. I watched with fascination and anticipation. Men like Sergeant Blaketon, with a wealth of experience beneath their belts, could certainly teach youngsters like me how to deal with the great British public. I had a lot to learn.

I observed him striding confidently towards the house, but as he approached, I noticed the familiar grey hair and beard emerge from an upstairs window. I did not shout a warning – I couldn't, for I was in the car some distance away, but Charlie must have said something to the striding sergeant because he halted in his tracks and looked up at the bedroom window.

I saw the barrel of the shotgun appear across the window sill, and it was quite evident that Charlie was issuing threatening words towards my sergeant. It was equally clear that my sergeant thought he was joking.

As a multitude of past visitors had come to appreciate, the Recluse of Rannockdale never joked with people who trespassed on his land, even if they were clad in the resplendent uniform of a British police sergeant. Having given Sergeant Blaketon his marching orders, and having had those orders repudiated by a stubborn, rule-bound sergeant, Charlie resorted to the only means at his disposal. He pulled the trigger.

A barrage of lead shot spattered the ground alarmingly close to Sergeant Blaketon's feet and it caused lots of little eruptions of earth. It was rapidly followed by a second barrel, at which more earth erupted about Sergeant Blaketon. Charlie shouted something at him and I saw Sergeant Blaketon change his mind about staying to talk. I saw him do something I've never seen him do before or since. He started to run.

To see a figure of the majesty of Oscar Blaketon in full flight with repeated barrages of lead pellets spurring him on his way, is indeed a rare sight. It was more so because he was holding his cap on with one hand and clutching the firearms certificate renewal forms in the other. He reached the car by leaping across the gate with a single bound, and he collapsed at my side as I moved into the driving seat. He was panting like a broken-winded horse, and perspiration was swilling down his cheeks and neck. I've never seen him in such a state of panic, and his breathing was tortuous as he signalled me to drive rapidly away. I drove off and saw the grey-haired old buzzard waving his gun in triumph.

'The man's an idiot,' Sergeant Blaketon gasped when he regained some of his breath. 'An absolute idiot. I'll get him certified, Rhea, so I will.'

He lapsed into a long silence as I drove steadily back to Ashfordly where I knew his wife would have his lunch ready. He didn't speak any more until I pulled into the police station car park.

'Rhea, if you mention this to anybody, I'll have you transferred to Gunnerside.'

And with that parting remark, he walked away, not quite so erect and certainly more dishevelled than he had been at the start of this enterprise. I wondered what I had learned from his demonstration of human understanding, but I never told a soul about it.

Chapter 6

'It is a silly game where nobody wins.'
THOMAS FULLER (1608–1661)

IT WOULD BE REMISS of me to suggest that a rural policeman's job is all work and no play. Certainly, in my time as a village constable the position demanded a twenty-four-hour responsibility even though our duty sheets showed that we worked eight-hour shifts. In truth, an eight-hour day was a rarity because people called or rang with problems, and it was understood that we attended to all matters that came our way, even though we were officially off duty or on leave.

Only for special tasks were we instructed to work more than eight hours. The public didn't know this – they simply arrived at the door to complain of being raped or robbed and we had to attend. To win time off in lieu, however, was most difficult. Supervisory checks were made of our daily tally of hours worked and woe betide us if we were shown to have worked less than an eight-hour day. The bits we worked over the eight were lost to us; we donated them to the uncaring public.

Even so, we were allocated days off duty. On the duty sheets, they were shown as RD which means Rest Day, and they moved forward two at a time, being Monday/Tuesday one week, Wednesday/Thursday the next, Friday/Saturday after that, with Sunday/Monday to follow, *ad infinitum*. As this ritual progressed, it became a great achievement to secure a Saturday/Sunday weekend off duty. On this kind of rota system, Saturday/Sunday weekends came around very infrequently, and were consequently cherished as a gift from the gods, or perhaps from Sergeant Blaketon. In practice, however, something always happened to cause our Saturday/Sunday weekends to be altered. Some incident would occur through which it became necessary to work on those sacred days, and this served only to galvanise us into positive action designed to secure that cherished time off.

Sergeant Blaketon was noted for his ability to find excuses to cancel our weekends off. He had a thing about policemen working when no one else did, such as Sunday evenings, Monday mornings very early, Good Fridays and a host of other occasions which he dredged from his years of compiling police duty sheets. He appeared to think it was good for us. After a while, we learned to tolerate his quirks and we came around to the notion of never expecting a proper weekend off. When one did arrive, it was a bonus rather than a right, and we all know how pleasant it is to receive the occasional bonus.

Through working almost every Saturday/Sunday, however, the discerning constable begins to yearn for a weekend off and contemplates the best ways of getting his weekends free. One of those ways was, and still is, to participate in police sport. Basing my logic on the understanding that if you can't beat 'em, join 'em, I renewed my acquaintanceship with the sporting section of my local constabulary.

Being a Yorkshireman, this meant playing cricket. All Yorkshiremen are supposed to play cricket and any who fail to reach a passable stage in this most remarkable of rural games are not considered genuine Yorkshiremen. I had reasoned that if I wanted a Saturday off duty now and again, to be with my growing family, the easiest guarantee was to join the Divisional Cricket Team. If I did this, I would be sent to play at selected rural pitches within our Division, and I could take along my wife and four tiny supporters. We'd all get an airing.

With this devious plan at the back of my mind, I singled out the cricket captain of our Division. I had to wait several weeks in the spring, but one fine April evening, I came across him in Eltering Police Station. I had popped in to record someone's production of an insurance certificate and driving licence. Sergeant Alex Benwell was there, checking some Court Sheets. He was my passport to free weekends.

'Evening, Sergeant,' I removed my cap and hung it on a peg near the back entrance, trusting my greeting was affable and warm.

'Now, lad,' he grunted while fingering down a long list of defendants due to appear at next week's Eltering Magistrates' Court.

I felt it unwise to disturb him for he was clearly engaged upon a matter of grave importance, but he broke the ice by saying, 'Put the kettle on, will you?'

'Yes, Sergeant,' I acquiesced for the sake of free Saturdays. In no time, the leaky station kettle was singing and I had found some stained mugs and a tin containing tea leaves. I produced a useful brew in an earthenware teapot with a cracked spout, and waited for him to leave his Court Sheets. Soon he came into the tiny rest room, smiled and sat on a rickety chair.

'Now, lad,' he said for the second time. 'Good brew,

is it?'

'Like my mother makes,' I said, realising he had no idea what sort of tea my mother makes. I poured a generous mugful which he inspected carefully before sipping noisily.

'Not bad,' he said. 'Aye, not bad at all. Your mother sounds as though she knows summat about making tea.'

'She likes a strong pot,' I agreed. 'The sort that a spoon can stand up in.'

He laughed loudly, 'Aye, we used to call it tonsil varnish when I was in the Army. It was powerful stuff.'

He sipped again, and then eyed me carefully. 'Rhea, isn't it?'

'Yes, Sergeant. I'm at Aidensfield, the new man there.'

'You sound like a Yorkshireman?' he said, his heavy face studying me.

'I am,' I confirmed with deep pride. 'Born and bred in Eskdale, I'm as Yorkshire as anyone can be.'

'Then you'll play cricket,' he said by way of a statement rather than a question.

He'd introduced the subject! Him, not me. I recognised my golden opportunity to get into the team.

'Yes,' I said confidently. 'I was captain of our village lads' team, and used to play in the second team as an adult.'

I daren't admit I'd never scored more than fifteen, and wasn't a very good fielder or bowler …

'If you're a Yorkshireman,' he was saying, 'you'll do for us. Next Saturday? What are you doing next Saturday?'

'Has the season started?' I asked.

'Week after,' he slurped his tea and smacked his

lips. 'By, you make a sound brew, young man. Next week, we're practising. Down at Eltering nets here, on the town playing fields. Saturday afternoon.'

'I'm on late turn,' I told him. 'That rules me out.'

'Who allocated that shift to a cricketer?' he bellowed. 'No cricketer gets a late turn on a Saturday. I'll have words with old Blaketon. From now on, you don't work late on Saturdays. So be at the nets at two o'clock.'

'Yes, Sergeant, but suppose Sergeant Blaketon won't change my duties?'

'He will,' was all he said, draining the dregs with his customary noise. 'Thanks for the tea, lad. What's your first name?'

'Nick,' I said.

'Nick,' he repeated, getting up from his chair. He was a massive man with a huge girth and legs like tree trunks. He almost waddled from the tea room, but his jovial face revealed a soft, gentle nature beneath his hard exterior. He seldom visited our stations, for he was the town sergeant over at Staddleton, a market town just inside our Divisional boundaries. Only infrequently did he venture into our Section, and I'd been fortunate enough to meet him.

I found myself wondering how he could run and field, for men of this size were notably ungainly, and he seemed to move with ponderous lethargy across the office. But he was a contact worth cultivating and I chattered away to him, discussing the job and his views on how rural bobbies should operate. He talked a lot of sense and I liked him from the start.

Later that evening, I met Sergeant Blaketon at a point in Thackerston, and told him all was quiet. I must be brave and broach the subject of cricket ...

'Oh,' I said, hoping my expression would excuse the nature of my forthcoming request. 'Oh, Sergeant, I met Sergeant Benwell at Eltering earlier this evening.'

He eyed me with considerable suspicion.

'And?' He gazed at me through those dark eyes and fierce eyebrows, his face not revealing one iota of his thoughts.

'He wants me to play cricket for the Divisional team,' I rushed out the words, 'and says he wants me to attend practice at Eltering nets next Saturday afternoon.'

'Did he now?'

He lapsed into an unhealthy silence, and I didn't know how to continue. Was I supposed to press home my point?

I waited for what seemed an eternity and decided I must make the next move. 'He asked if you would change my duties,' I said weakly.

'Rhea, you ought to know better than listen to Alex Benwell. You know what he's like ...'

'Like?' I asked, innocently.

'Yes, like. You've seen him? The size of him?'

I nodded.

'Beer. That's the result of years of drinking gallons of beer, and all at cricket matches. Cricket's not a sport for him, Rhea, it's an excuse to go boozing on a Saturday night. That's how he gets out of Saturday night duties, Rhea; puts it all down to sport. Just because the Superintendent's a member of the Yorkshire Cricket Club ... you didn't approach him, then? You didn't seek him out to fix this for you?'

'No, Sergeant.'

'Not like some I know,' he said without halting for breath. 'Some less honourable members of this section always wheedle their way into the cricket team to avoid Saturday duties, Rhea. It means the rest of us, me included, have to do their duties for them, week in and week out …'

'He asked if I could attend the nets, Sergeant. I suppose he wants to see me play.'

'All right, if that's all. Nets it is. Next Saturday – you don't play football, do you?'

'Not really, Sergeant,' I had to admit.

'Now that's my game, Rhea. Pure English football. I play football in the winter, you know. To keep fit. That's a real game, a real sport, a real contest …'

He was making a note in his pocket book, reminding himself to change the duty sheets. 'Don't make this a habit, Rhea. I know you are not a skiver who wants only to have each Saturday off …'

'No, Sergeant, not at all. It's just that Sergeant Benwell suggested it …'

'I don't like that man,' said Sergeant Blaketon, closing his book. He drove away with a heavy and worried frown on his handsome face.

I enjoyed my session at the nets. There would be some fifteen off-duty policemen there, all testing their new boots, their freshly laundered whites and their muscles. I had a go at bowling and found my old skills returning, although my efforts with a bat weren't particularly promising. I fielded one or two nice balls and spent a very enjoyable three hours. Mary had come with me, chiefly for the outing in our car with the family, and the three elder ones spent the afternoon running about while I kept half an eye on them. Mary and the baby popped into town to do some shopping.

It wasn't a bad arrangement, but Mary was quite firm about accompanying me. She was determined to come with me upon every trip because it would give her a Saturday outing with me, and in some senses it would make our life resemble that of normal weekend people.

However, the outcome of my first practice was that I was selected for the Divisional Police team to play in the Ryedale League. Our opponents would be teams from the villages of the district. Because the police had no home ground, we begged and borrowed fields from other clubs and because Eltering was the most central, we were allowed to use it whenever Eltering had an away game. That became our Home ground, the Away grounds being remote villages and hamlets in the moors and dales.

It would be impossible to describe the sheer enjoyment we experienced at those villages, but our match against Brantgate First Eleven one Saturday in June typifies our experiences. This can be taken as the sort of match in which we engaged. It was an Away match for us, which meant we had to tolerate Brantgate's unique pitch. I had never played there, but my colleagues assured me a treat was in store.

Sergeant Benwell collected several of us at Eltering Police Station and I was surprised to find myself being transported in a battered old ambulance. This was his cricket coach, the vehicle he used to ferry himself and his pals to distant matches. Mary had decided not to come because Elizabeth was feeling off colour, so I decided to travel with the others and give her the use of our car, should she need it.

The retired ambulance rumbled and rolled across the countryside and we climbed steeply into the depths of the moors. Half an hour later, we were trundling merrily across the heights with staggering views spread below our lofty route. We could look down upon a multitude of deep valleys and admired the sheer breathtaking splendour of it all. The glaciers of old had done a wonderful sculpture job on those hills.

'Down here,' announced Alex Benwell, as he turned into a narrow lane. His route dropped sharply from elevated moorland road, turned left down the sheer side of a valley, then twisted and wove between high drystone walls. We drove slowly down the 1-in-3 gradient, the old truck groaning in low gear towards the bottom. Down there nestled the hamlet of Brantgate, a sleepy moorland collection of farms and cottages.

Suddenly, we rounded a blind corner and there, right across the road, was a five-bar gate. Its purpose was to prevent the free-ranging moorland sheep from invading the village gardens, and as we approached it, Sergeant Benwell pressed his foot on the brake. Nothing. Nothing happened.

'Brakes have gone!' he shouted as we began to gather speed. The monster gate loomed closer and I saw him grip the steering wheel firmly between both hands. Then I felt the ancient vehicle rapidly accelerate. He'd put his foot on the accelerator and we roared towards the stout gate. The nose of the heavy vehicle rammed it amidships, and the gate flew open with a crash. The force of it sent the latch flying over one wall and while the gate stood wide open for a fraction of a second, we hurtled through. The gate, as if on springs, rebounded from the wall and slammed shut. But we were through and were now careering headlong down the continuing gradient. Benwell knew the road and he was a first-class driver; he had to be, to guide the brakeless old truck down this steep, winding lane. By the grace of God, nothing was coming up the hill; there was no room to pass even a bike. By knowing his vehicle so well, and being such a fine steersman, he suddenly turned the wheel and we roared off the road into a long field. He allowed the low gears to control the forward rush and after about a hundred yards, the ambulance eased to a smooth halt. Seven cricketers emerged, some feeling sick and others marvelling at his motoring skills. But Benwell was unruffled.

He kicked the front wheels and said calmly, 'It's never done that before,' then walked off to the pavilion.

We followed, the other police players having made their own way to Brantgate. The pavilion was little more than a decorated hen-house, but we managed to change into our whites and find somewhere to spread open the cricket bag with its pads, balls, bats, bails and score book. As we busied ourselves for a practice session, the Brantgate captain came in.

'Now then,' he said gruffly. 'Most of you fellers are newcomers, aren't you?'

'Eight or nine of 'em,' confirmed Alex Benwell, tying his laces.

'Then you'd better come with me,' said the captain, 'and I'll explain the rules.'

'Rules?' I queried, wondering if I had heard the word correctly. I was under the impression that all games of cricket were played with the same rules.

'Local rules,' said Alex Benwell. 'Go out and listen to him.'

We obeyed and the dour Yorkshireman, whose cricket gear comprised a white shirt and grey flannels fortified by a pair of stained white boots, led us away. We followed through long grass for a considerable distance and he halted on a neatly shorn piece of land. It was twenty-two yards long by about ten feet wide.

All around was long grass, knee high in places and I noted the outfield was surrounded by an electric fence. Furthermore, it was impossible to see one of the boundaries because the pitch had been hewn out of a steep sloping hillside. The pitch was the only flat part of the field; above it, the outfield rose steeply towards a wooden fence several yards distant, and the electric fence was mid-way up that slope.

'Now then,' said the captain. 'I'm Jake Foston, captain of this team. This is our cricket pitch – I allus fetches new lads out to have a look at it because it's not a normal one. It's a good pitch, mind, takes spin very well and is as level as a billiard table top. Our lads have done some good work. But yon outfield is a bit brant.'

I knew this was the dialect word for steep, and could see how the village got its name.

'Now, we can't help that. Nature's made this field and nature's got to be respected. Out in mid-field there's an electric fence, that's to keep cows off this pitch. It's switched off now, but you'll have to watch it if you have to chase a ball. Leap over it if you can – it's nobbut a couple of foot high. Beyond that there's the real boundary, and yon railings mark it. Through there is six.'

'You mean over there, surely?' asked someone from our side.

'Nay, through is six. If a ball goes through there, our lads could run ten or fifteen while you find t'ball among t'nettles. So we play fair and allow six. If you clout it *over* that fence, then it's eight.'

I began to wonder what sort of signals the umpires would use to signify these scores, and also how our scorer would record these runs, but Jake thundered on.

'Down t'hill,' he said, 'you'll not see t'boundary

because it's out o'sight. You'll need a feller down there to call back the score. He'll have to be a bit sharp because he'll not be able to see t'batsmen nor can he know when t'ball's heading his way. So you lads will have to yell at him. "Ball's coming," or summat like that. "Left or right a bit." He'll soon cotton on.'

Jake paused to allow us to think about that part of the game, then he continued, 'Beyond yon electric fence there's lots of cow-claps. If a ball goes in one and stops there, we give you five runs. That's to let you have time to wipe it clean before chucking it back at your wicket-keeper and we reckon that's fair. Cow-claps are five. That hen-house,' and he indicated a hen-house tucked in the upper corner, 'if you clout that hen-house it's a six. If it goes inside, it's eight.'

'It won't be easy, fielding in this long grass,' a policeman player said, guardedly.

'No, it's not, but we're used to it,' smiled Jake. 'And we can't cut it just for a cricket match or two, our cows need feeding, and this is good cow grass.'

We followed upon a brief circuit of this unique cricket field and had no alternative but to agree with Brantgate's interpretation of the rules. We were assured that their scorer, who would sit in the pavilion alongside ours, would keep us informed, and that he was an honest as a new babe.

'Now,' he said, 'there's one other thing.'

We waited with bated breath.

'We're a team member short, lads, one of our best players had to rush off to hospital with his missus. She's calving, he reckons, and he had to take her on his tractor.'

I tried to visualise the farmer's pregnant wife sitting on a tractor and being rushed off to the maternity ward.

I also wondered what the hospital authorities would make of it when the pair arrived.

'So?' asked Alex Benwell.

'We've a player to stand in for him, from another team.'

'I've no objections, have you?' Alex faced us.

We all shook our heads.

'Then that's him,' and the host team's captain pointed to a sturdy farmer in his sixties. Ebenezer Flintoft wore thick hobnailed boots, corduroy trousers lashed around the knees with bits of string, a thick working shirt with no collar and the sleeves rolled above his elbows, red braces and a flat cap. He beamed at us as we stared at him, and I noticed his mouth was devoid of teeth. He needed a shave too, for his chin bristled with grey hairs.

'It's t'father-in-law of our opening bat,' announced Jake. 'He's over for t'day, helping out with some pigs, but said he'd help us out if we were stuck.'

We agreed to this last-minute substitution, but didn't really see that it mattered. The fellow was clearly a non-cricketer and had come along as a goodwill gesture.

The rules having been explained, we tossed and lost. Jake elected to bat, and I knew why. We'd have an awful job coping with stray balls in that outfield, and so we did. They knocked our bowling all over the field, causing the ball to get stuck in cow-claps, to get fast in the hedge, to get lost in long grass, and to vanish over that hidden boundary below us.

It is difficult, due to the passage of time, to highlight the most memorable aspects of that enjoyable game, but one character does stand out above all the others. It was the last-minute addition, Ebenezer Flintoft with his flat cap, hobnailed boots and braces.

He came in at No. 5 and we then realised their best batsmen had performed. If they were putting Ebenezer in to bat at this early stage, the remainder must be rubbish. Sergeant Benwell decided to give our opening bowler another crack at them, fully expecting him to skittle out the remainder for a very low score.

But they had expected nothing like Ebenezer. He flung the bat around like lightning, hitting everything that moved. He kept scoring fours, sixes and eights with monotonous regularity, and nothing seemed to beat him. He was very evidently having a whale of a time. The others came and went, but Ebenezer returned to the pavilion not out and beaming all over his whiskery face. 'By gum,' he said, 'I right enjoyed yon knock about. How many did I get?' He'd scored 125 out of a total of 187.

We broke the proceedings for tea, and it was magnificent. The wives of the Brantgate team laid on a gorgeous tea worthy of any moorland funeral, and we resumed the game shortly after five o'clock. We didn't stand a chance of reaching their score, although sixes and eights could soon rattle up a useful total.

Sergeant Benwell was our opening batsman and I was amazed to see that Ebenezer was their opening bowler. The large, heavy Yorkshireman took a short run, whirled his arm in a peculiar sideways motion and delivered a ball that utterly beat poor old Benwell.

By some good luck, he survived the first over and began to score off the second bowler, but when Ebenezer returned, I could see that poor old Sergeant Benwell was struggling. He was clean bowled with the fourth ball of the second over, and this signified our impending collapse.

We did manage a creditable 56, all scored off the other bowlers, because Ebenezer was totally unplayable. We limped back to the pavilion, beaten and trounced by this village team from the moors.

But they treated us well. We were invited to the local pub for a friendly drink, and the blacksmith did something to Sergeant Benwell's brakes which made his old truck mobile once again. The way home was jolly and happy as we sang loud songs and told countless jokes. I certainly enjoyed that day's cricket, and all that followed.

I was to learn later that Ebenezer played for most of the moorland village teams. He lived in an isolated farm which did not belong to any village, consequently he was invited to play in several teams. He invariably won the match when they played outsiders, and I wondered how the teams coped if he was supposed to play for both. Knowing how these fellows played, he probably did play for both sides, just to even things out!

Some weeks later, I was chatting to a farmer from the moors and mentioned that match, with special reference to Ebenezer's role.

'Aye, Mr Rhea,' he said, 'if awd Ebenezer had taken t'game seriously, he might have been some good at it.'

I did not play cricket every Saturday, for my performances were by no means memorable. I was unreliable as a batsman, erratic as a fielder and moderately useful as a bowler, so I played only when the best could not be spared from their shifts and unexpected duties. But I enjoyed my games. They did provide me with several opportunities to take Mary and the family into the country and they did introduce me to other members of our widespread Division. The social life was fine.

My own sport, which I had practised as a youngster before marriage, was cycle racing. It was not a sport which was encouraged within the police force, and I sold my trusty drop-handlebar special ten-speed lightweight Tour de France model. I could never envisage myself aboard such a machine in full uniform, with my backside elevated, my head down and my big boots turning lightweight pedals. This meant I no longer partook in cycle races or time-trials.

Furthermore, I never expected to use my cycling skills in the police force, but one night, I was instructed to take the Ashfordly official police cycle and patrol the main road. The reason was that the county car had broken down and my motorcycle was due for a service. And so it was with great amusement that Sergeant Bairstow allocated me a cycle beat from 10 p.m. until 2 a.m.

I found the huge black monster and trundled it from the garage, where I dusted it down and tested things like tyres, brakes and lights. Everything worked well, thanks to the immaculate attention of PC Alwyn Foxton. He kept everything in fine working order. With some trepidation, therefore, I mounted the massive cycle with its double crossbar and straight handlebars and sallied forth upon my cycle patrol. It was, in truth, the very first, and indeed only, cycle patrol I performed in my career.

It wasn't long before I was enjoying the experience. I could feel the wind against my cheeks and I enjoyed the solitude and silence. Memories flooded back as I pressed those heavy pedals round and round.

I patrolled the main road and took little sojourns into the lanes at the side of the highway, calling at villages and inspecting out-of-the-way lock up properties while on patrol. I had lost a little of my racing ability but the old techniques soon returned as I steered the heavy cycle about its business. I found hill climbing difficult because of the straight handlebars, and found the heavy gears rather clumsy but a bonus did occur due to the weight of the cycle. Once I had encouraged it to speed along in top gear, its own momentum kept it going and it was possible to reach a moderately high rate of knots. I liked this sensation, and concluded that Sergeant Bairstow had unwittingly done me a favour tonight.

I paused at a telephone kiosk to make a midnight point and as I stood in the silence, I heard the distinctive swish of oncoming tyres. Another cyclist was approaching – could it be Sergeant Bairstow?

I peered from behind my kiosk and saw the approaching light. It was weaving slightly from side to side as the cyclist pressed towards the conclusion of his journey, and when he passed me, I noticed it was a racing cyclist. He had his head low over the handlebars and was clad in all-black gear, comprising a sweat shirt and shorts, topped by a black cap. The cycle was a racing machine, and I guessed he was clocking himself to compete in a time-trial at some future date.

But as he passed my vantage point, I saw that his back light was not working. As he rode away from me, he was rapidly lost in the darkness and his black clothing made him virtually invisible. The fellow was a risk to himself and to motorists, and I could foresee an accident of a horrible kind. I imagined some motorist running into the rear of this cyclist and killing him, or at the least severely injuring him.

'Hey!' I shouted, emerging from my waiting place. 'Hey, stop!'

There was no response. The cyclist kept his head down and tore away into the night.

Not liking to be ignored, and angry that my call had been unheeded, I mounted my trusty old police cycle and gave chase. The heavy machine seemed like a tank, and it took an awful lot of pedal pressure to persuade it to move at speed. But within a few minutes, I was hurtling along in pursuit of the unlit cycle, hell-bent on reporting this thoughtless character for riding without lights.

The thrill of the chase spurred me to great efforts, and I felt as if I was riding in a time-trial, striving to catch up with the chap who would have one full minute's start on me. But this character had only a few seconds lead, and I succeeded. My own headlight caught the reflection of his pedals and I urged my sturdy steed to even greater efforts as I drew closer.

'Hey!' I shouted. 'Police, stop!'

I was panting by this time, but my legs were holding out and I was certainly drawing closer to him. 'Hey, you!' I began to call. 'Police, stop!'

The fellow did not respond. His head was low over the handlebars as he pressed his pedals and I thought he was trying to get away from me. I called upon my reserves and all my past cycling skills as I forced the old police bike to draw level with him.

'Hey!' I shouted across at him, for I could see his ears now. 'Hey, stop. Police.'

He looked across at me and I could see the pain and anguish of competition on his face.

'What is it?' he panted.

'That back light of yours. It's not working. I've been trying to halt you … you ignored my orders …'

'Look,' he said. 'I'm sorry. I didn't hear you,' and he continued to forge ahead. 'I'm in a desperate hurry, Officer, can't you see? I'm breaking a record …'

'A record?'

'Doing a fifty,' he said in racing jargon. 'I've only a mile to go … I daren't stop …'

'You're a danger to yourself!' I shouted, but my cycling days had also taught me the agony of attempting to better one's own time, and the thrill of breaking other people's records.

'I daren't lose precious seconds fixing that light,' he pleaded, head down again. 'Please bear with me, it's not far now.'

'You could get killed,' I snapped, and then I realised I could help him.

'One more mile, officer, then I've done it … the fifty record will be mine, I'm ahead on time.'

'Right,' I decided. 'Keep going. I'll tuck in behind you, and my light will act as a warning. Keep going, and don't flag …'

And I moved into his slipstream. I followed him for that final mile, he breaking some record and me urging the old police bike to its utmost speed as I kept pace with the record breaker. Towards the end, I knew he was flagging; I most certainly was, but I think my presence immediately behind helped to keep him going. After all, it would look rather odd if a fully uniformed policeman on a police cycle crossed the line ahead of him, so I reckon I did him a service.

He achieved his record by knocking some 50 seconds off the local record and he thanked me for my help. He fixed his light – the bulb had worked loose and I did not report him. I doubt if I could have spoken the necessary words. It took an age to regain my breath and cool down.

I did wonder how that old bike would have performed over the full fifty miles, but decided against making the attempt.

After all, a quick sprint over one mile is exhilarating, even on a police cycle, but it would have been impossible to sustain that pace for much longer. He deserved his record.

If there was one sport in which I had no interest, it was Association Football. I had played at school but completely failed to understand the off-side rule. In my teens, I had never felt inclined to attend Saturday afternoon matches, either of the village variety or at Middlesbrough which was then a top-class First Division team. Consequently, upon my appointment as a constable I had never expressed the slightest interest in playing football for my division, my station or the village team. Even if this did promise time off on Saturday, less night duty and more beer swilling, the appeal of the sport in all its facets was lost on me.

Following my first cricket season, therefore, I was somewhat horrified when Sergeant Blaketon sidled up to me one Wednesday morning and asked, 'Rhea, are you busy on Saturday?'

In my mind, this was a loaded question. I was supposed to be on Rest Day, and I knew that Mary was hoping for an outing of some kind; if I said I was busy, he'd ask what it was, and if I said I wasn't busy, he was likely to put me on night duty.

'Why, Sergeant?' I replied with a question, a useful form of defence.

'I need help, Rhea,' I detected the tone of a plaintive cry in his voice.

'What sort of help, Sergeant?' I was still being very guarded.

'I note you are on Rest Day, Rhea,' he said, his eyes swivelling towards the duty sheet which was pinned to the wall, 'and I thought if you hadn't anything special to do, you might come to my rescue. After all, I did allow you to play cricket.'

'If it is something serious, Sergeant,' I heard myself saying, 'I'll be only too pleased to help.'

'It is very serious,' he informed me sternly. 'You've heard of the Ashfordly Veterans' Club Football Team?'

'No,' I said truthfully, not being a football fanatic.

'I thought you were a sportsman, Rhea?' he put to me. 'All this cricket and that cycling of yours.'

'I wouldn't call myself a sportsman, Sergeant,' I admitted. 'What's this got to do with the Veterans?'

He coughed. 'I am playing for the Veterans this season,' he flushed ever so slightly. 'In fact,' he smiled weakly, 'I'm captain.'

'Congratulations.' I didn't know what to say, or what I was expected to say.

'This Saturday is a very important game,' he went on. 'We are playing in the final of the Ryedale Veterans' League Challenge Cup, here at Ashfordly Sports Ground. It's against the Brantsford side.'

I wondered if he wanted me to write up an account of the match for the local paper, or to act as linesman maybe?

'You're playing too?' I smiled.

'I'm in goal,' he said proudly. 'My old position. When I was a young man, Rhea, I was a crack goalkeeper. My height was useful and I kept for the Force on twenty occasions; indeed I was short-listed for the British Police Football Team, as goalkeeper.'

'Then your team will have no trouble winning,' I beamed at him. I had no idea that he'd been so skilled and he must have been outstanding to have been short-listed for the British team.

'We're a man short,' he said quickly. 'Full back. I wondered if you would play for us?'

'Me?' I laughed. 'Sergeant, I've never played football since I was at school. I hardly know one end of a pitch from the other.'

'I can't find anyone. We're short as a general rule, but this weekend it's desperate. Two of our members have gone down with rheumatism, and one's got flu. We can't play unless we turn out a full team.'

'But I'm not a veteran!' I protested. 'I'm only twenty-six.'

'Anyone over twenty-five qualifies,' he beamed. 'That's a rule, I checked before asking you.'

To put it mildly, I was talked into playing for Sergeant Blaketon's creaking team. Mary laughed and said she would attend the game, for she could do with a good laugh. The thought of me running around a football pitch, however amateurish the game, was more than a giggle – it was hilarious.

That Saturday afternoon, therefore, I reported to Ashfordly Sports Ground and found Sergeant Blaketon prancing up and down in a dark blue jumper and white shorts. My kit was in the changing room, and it was the same colour. As I changed, I felt awful; the men around me, most of whom were in their forties and very fit, were clearly addicts of the game and I hoped Oscar Blaketon had acquainted them with my total lack of know-how. If youth was on my side, experience was not.

I remember where full-backs were supposed to play, having dredged that fact deep from my school memories and I swotted up something of the game in one of my reference books. I also learned that Blaketon's team had conquered all competitors prior to this game. This was the final. The thought that the fate of the League Challenge Cup lay at my feet was horrifying. I had agonised for hours before the game, worrying myself sick as to why he had selected me and what I'd done wrong to find myself in this awful position. The duty sheet told me – the three best footballers of the Section were all on duty, and Oscar could hardly change their duties to play when he'd been so critical of the cricketers and their time off. Local police politics were very much in evidence on this occasion. None of the civilians in town were interested in the game – they were too busy watching professional matches or doing their own Saturday things. Such a lot depended upon me.

In the changing rooms, he rallied his team and welcomed me to the game, never mentioning my amateurism. He punched a few pieces of advice at them, and spent time telling them about his favourite moves, his tactics, the weaknesses in the opposition and the strengths of their forward line. He did a good job, I felt, for he managed to demoralise me totally. I stood with the others, goose-pimples on my legs and a lump in my throat, as the clock's pointers ticked irrevocably towards two-thirty.

Then we were running on to the pitch. I kicked a spare ball around, and leapt up and down like the others. I tried to head one or two practice shots, but missed the lot and before I knew what was happening, we were lining up for the kick-off.

I was nicely out of the way in my full-back position, but the opposing team looked ominous and threatening. Brantsford Veterans had the reputation of being a formidable side, and as we lined up, they galloped noisily around the pitch in their bright red strip, threatening us with total annihilation. Sergeant Blaketon won the toss and elected to play into the wind, hoping they would tire themselves out by the time they had to do likewise. Then he made his way between the clean white goalposts, there to defend the reputation of Ashfordly Veterans.

I noticed that everyone was trotting on the spot so I did the same, then the whistle blew. It shrilled loudly, and I started to run about knowing that in the very near future, I would have to attempt to stop the onward rush of the opposition. I was the last line of defence before the goal, and Oscar Blaketon was in goal, I couldn't let him down. I daren't let him down.

The first half went rapidly. I kicked the ball several times which made me feel moderately useful, and I didn't appear to do anything that caused groans and contempt from the others. In fact, one of my shots landed right at the feet of our centre forward and he raced towards the goal, being narrowly defeated on his run. I was congratulated because I had almost made a goal, and I felt proud. I could see Mary on the touchline, mingling with the handful of spectators, and she applauded that piece of skill. Suddenly I felt confidence flowing through my veins.

By half-time, I was feeling even better. My patrol duties and my cricket during the summer had kept me fit and the exercise was not too strenuous. Age was on my side and I found I could outrun most of the Brantsford team members, although I must admit their skills were infinitely greater than mine. But I enjoyed the first half and walked off the field feeling very pleased. I waved to Mary as I entered the changing room for a drink of orange and a towelling.

The score was nil-nil at this stage, and everything

depended upon the second half. We were now playing with the wind, an undoubted asset and I could sense Sergeant Blaketon's confidence as we took to the field for the second half.

We were certainly the fitter team. In that second half, we ran rings around their men, and I thoroughly enjoyed myself. I raced up field with the ball and kicked it to our own men time and time again, our efforts being thwarted only by the anticipation and good luck of their goalkeeper. Time and time again he saved powerful shots, and then one of their men fouled our centre forward.

It was a dirty foul, the action of a desperate man, and our player fell to the ground in agony as his shin took the force of a well-aimed kick. My team exploded with anger because our man had been racing towards the goal as the goalie had come forward to vacate his position. We couldn't fail to score – then we were fouled. The referee awarded a free kick, not a penalty and I didn't know enough about the game to worry about the difference, but it angered our lads. Shouts and cat-calls filled the air and Sergeant Blaketon had a difficult job calming them down. The tension was intolerable.

But Blaketon succeeded. As our centre forward hobbled off the pitch with his leg bleeding nastily, we were compelled to continue with ten men. There were no substitutes. We had about thirty-five minutes to play before full time, and while our earlier efforts should have produced results, it was now doubtful whether we could maintain that pressure. The centre forward, a butcher called Andy Storr, was a gallant and skilled team member and he would be missed. Their viciousness had hit us where it hurt most.

When all the fuss had died away, the game resumed and quite suddenly, I had the ball. I have no idea how it arrived at my feet, for I was still angry about the foul, but I thought of Sergeant Blaketon and the honour that could be his. Forgetting I was a full-back, I side-stepped a player who tackled me and tore down the right wing with the ball bouncing at my feet. I felt the thrill of the chase as players milled around and tackled me; I saw Mary on the touchline, her hands waving and her voice calling to me, and I flew across the grass. Nothing could stop me now; I was on wings of happiness and success.

Someone attempted to intercept me, and I did a quick body-swerve to deposit him on the ground as I continued my racing run. Never before had I experienced such a thrill and I could hear the cheers of the spectators as I raced towards the goal. I beat all comers; I was in a haze as I switched into skills I never knew I possessed. I thought of Sergeant Blaketon and the cup, my eyes filled with tears of happiness as I raced those final yards to the goal. I was unstoppable. Then a hush descended. The ground bore an air of expectancy and I knew it all depended on me.

I was before the goalkeeper; he crouched between the posts and my misty eyes could distinguish his dark figure with arms outstretched as I took my careful aim.

I have never kicked a football with such power and accuracy. It flew from my right foot and the goalkeeper didn't stand a chance. He dived across the goalmouth in a desperate bid to beat my shot, but the driving ball crashed into the net with a resounding thud of leather against netting.

I wiped my eyes. I had done it. And me a full-back too!

'What the bloody hell are you doing, Rhea?' cried Sergeant Blaketon as he picked the ball from the back of the net. 'This is *our* goal!'

He didn't ask me to play again, for his team lost by that solitary goal, and I daren't ask him for time off to play cricket the following year.

He retired from football after that game, and I must admit I felt sorry for him.

I hope he didn't think I'd done it on purpose.

Chapter 7

'If you want to win her hand,
Let the maiden understand,
That she's not the only pebble on the beach.'
HARRY BRAISTED (19th century)

AS I SETTLED IN my office to compile the quarterly return of farms visited and inspections of stock registers, I discovered I had omitted one busy establishment. According to the record maintained in my office, my predecessor had called there at least once a quarter and I had been lax in not continuing the practice.

On that May morning, therefore, I decided to rectify matters. I began my journey on the little Francis Barnett with the fresh breezes of May stirring the blossomed trees and the growing grass along the lanes. May must be the most beautiful of the English months for the landscape is bursting with fresh life, with flowers, leaves, insects and birds, all enjoying the warmth that comes from the strengthening sun. To be paid for patrolling through such splendid environs is indeed a bonus, and I enjoyed my ride across the valley.

I was heading for Slape Wath Farm, a lonely homestead buried deep in the moors over by Whemmelby. I had to consult my Ordnance Survey map before leaving the house, but established that I had to descend the steep 1-in-3 hill into

Whemmelby, drive out towards the summit of Gallow Heights and turn left about a mile before reaching the Heights. This took me along an unmade track which climbed across the heathery landscape before descending dramatically into a small valley. Deep in the valley lay the homestead called Slape Wath Farm, so named because the track crossed the mountain stream near the farm, then wound its way across the moors, eventually leading to the main road from Eltering to Strensford. In our Yorkshire dialect, slape means slippery and a wath is water-splash or a ford, so the farm was aptly named. The crossing would be treacherous in winter.

I had to open several wooden gates, a tricky job with a motorcycle, but eventually found myself entering the yard of Slape Wath Farm. It was clean and nicely concreted, and I placed the machine against the wall of an outbuilding before walking across to the farm house. The time was shortly before eleven one Wednesday morning.

I halted before knocking on the door in order to check my records, and reminded myself of the occupants' names. The owners of this remote spread were the Misses Kirby, Frances and Irene to be precise. There was no other explanatory note in my records and I had never heard anyone mention these ladies; their farm, I appreciated, was far too remote for casual callers and I doubted if the two ladies in question enjoyed much of a social life.

My memory refreshed, I knocked on the kitchen door.

'A minute!' called a voice, and I waited. Presently, the door was opened and a huge masculine woman stood before me. She wore a hessian apron, a long working dress buttoned up to the neck and a curious dust-cap on her head. She was nearly six feet tall, with a head of ginger hair peeping beneath her headgear; her face was red with the effects of the weather but her eyes were unusually bright blue and bored into me as I stood on the doorstep. She was hefty and muscular, and wore heavy wellington boots which peeped beneath her long dress.

'Oh,' she said, eyeing me. 'It's t'policeman. Come in,' and she stepped back to permit me to enter. I noticed she had a large broom in her hands and she appeared to be in the middle of sweeping the sandstone floor of her kitchen.

'That's a useful brush,' I said by way of making an inane introductory comment.

'Aye,' she said, looking at it with pride. 'We've had it for thirty-five years, and all we've had for it is three new heads and two new shafts.'

I didn't know whether I was supposed to laugh at this statement as a joke or treat it as a piece of moorland feminine logic, but my embarrassment was avoided by the timely appearance of another lady. She was much smaller than the first but with the same ginger hair and masculine appearance. Her eyes were a paler blue and her face a trifle less colourful, but it was easy to deduce that the big lady was the man-about-the-farm, and her sister was the woman-about-the-house.

'I'm PC Rhea from Aidensfield,' I introduced myself. 'The new policeman.'

'Oh,' said the big one. 'Thoo'll be calling about our registers, then?'

'Yes,' I confirmed. 'I've been rather busy …'

'Think nowt on it, young man,' the big one said. 'Sit thyself down and Rene, fetch him a cuppa tea. Sugar?'

I shook my head and said, 'No thanks. Milk, no

sugar.'

'Mak it three, Rene,' ordered the big lady. 'Thoo come as well.'

Rene never spoke as she drifted across to an oven at the far end of this large kitchen and busied herself with pots, pans and bottles of milk. I placed my helmet on the scrubbed kitchen table and sat on a bench. The big lady, who I reasoned was called Frances, sat on the bench opposite and peered steadily at me.

'It'll be about them pigs, is it?' she put to me.

'You got some at Malton Mart last week,' I said. 'I've got to check to see everything's in order, and that you've entered them in your register.'

Without a word, she left her seat and went across to a cupboard hanging on the wall. She produced the register and flicked it open – an immaculate entry graced the pages and I said, 'I'll have to see the stock in question.'

'Thoo's a keen 'un, eh?' she grumbled, heading for the door.

'Just doing my job,' I said softy, following behind.

'We're off to t'sties, Rene!' she bellowed, her loud voice blasting my eardrums. 'Three minutes, no more.'

She led me in silence down to her pig sties and showed me the store pigs she'd bought. I leaned over the bottom half of the door, enjoying the sight of young pigs grunting in happiness as they nosed among the straw and potato peelings which covered the floor of their pen.

'Nice pigs,' I commented, for they were lovely.

'The best,' she said with some force. 'Me and our Rene nobbut buys t'best, thoo knaws. We show pigs and sheep, so we've got ti have t'best.'

'You show them?' I expressed interest in her remark. 'Do you win prizes?'

'Win prizes?' she bellowed. 'I'll say we win prizes. Great Yorkshire, Stokesley, Egton, Danby, Castleton, the Royal, you name it, and we've won there. We've got the best pigs this side of the Pennines.'

'You don't show these though?' I gestured towards those in the pig sty. 'These are for fattening, aren't they?'

'Aye, they are, young man. No, we breed our own show pigs.'

The kitchen door opened and the smaller edition said, 'Tea, Cis.'

'Tea, Constable,' said Cis striding towards the house with me almost trotting to keep pace. She led me inside. Rene had placed a green patterned oil cloth on the rough table, and there were three cups, some scones, jam, butter, three slabs of fruit cake and a pile of chocolate biscuits.

This was a typical 'lowance, as they called it here; tea break is the word elsewhere, or elevenses. To these folk, it's 'lowance time, or allowance time.

'Thank you, ladies,' I settled down and signed the book with a flourish. 'You keep a very nice tidy farm.'

'We've a man in,' said Cis. 'Jack Holtby.'

'He's employed full time, is he?'

'He lives in, Mr Rhea, gets fed and bedded here, all found. He looks after my pigs.'

'And my sheep,' said Rene quickly. 'Jack looks after my sheep as well.'

'She breeds sheep. I do the pigs.'

'They win at all the shows, Mr Rhea,' said Rene, getting into top gear now her tongue had been loosened. 'Good stock, is ours. You'll have heard of t'Kirbys of Whemmelby?'

I didn't know whether to acknowledge my ignorance by

152

shaking my head or to tell a white lie and pretend I knew all about their successes, but Frances saved the day by saying, 'Don't be stupid, Rene. Of course Mr Rhea knows about our showing. I've told him, and he reads the papers. Kirby's a famous name among showing folk; my pigs and your sheep are noted the country over.'

'I always get first with my blackfaces, Mr Rhea …'

'And me with my saddlebacks …'

I listened as the two sisters prattled on about their wins, each talking about her own speciality, and I began to realise I was witnessing a curious phenomenon. Once they left the subject of their pigs and sheep, their conversation followed a peculiar pattern. Each contributed to a sentence by apparently knowing what the other was going to say.

'They tell me you're married, Mr Rhea …'

'With four children, eh? How nice, your wife …'

'Must be very busy, looking after them and cooking and cleaning. Big families are nice, but …'

'I couldn't cope, not with four, not here. Animals are enough and …'

'They're just like children, keeping us out of bed at night and wanting feeding when …'

'They're little and in bed …'

'So we always work shifts, four hours on and four off, especially …'

'In the lambing season …'

And so it went on. I listened in amazement at this curious form of communication, and it appeared only to manifest itself when they were talking about subjects other than their pigs and sheep. It seemed that the pigs and sheep were individual matters, with Cis the big one looking after the pigs, and little Rene concentrating on

153

the sheep. I left the premises feeling very amused and wondered which of them was the elder. I guessed it was Cis, the larger of the pair, for she was the dominant one and certainly had the appearance of a man. It was difficult to estimate their ages – they could be anywhere between thirty-five and fifty, and I reckoned they were probably in their early forties.

During that visit, I did not see their man. Jack Holtby was nowhere to be seen, but evidence of his skills, or of their supervisory capacity, was everywhere. The farm was beautifully maintained; its woodwork was gleaming, its glasswork polished, the yards swept clean and the loose pieces of hay and straw tucked firmly into place. It was a picture of professionalism.

It would be about five weeks later when the name of these curious sisters cropped up in a casual conversation. I was in Aidensfield chattering to Joe Steel in his grocer's shop, and he asked, 'You'll have come across the Kirby twins, have you?'

'Twins?' I puzzled, and then remembered that Rene and Cis were called Kirby. 'You mean those ladies out at Slape Wath?'

'Aye, that's them. Twins. Rum lasses.'

I told him of my first visit to their establishment and of my fascination with their mode of speech. He laughed.

'They've always been like that, Mr Rhea. Get 'em talking about their own animals, and they'll be normal, but get off that subject and they both talk like one person. You should hear 'em in here, ordering groceries … one says, 'bread' and t'other says, 'butter', and they go on like that, right through a shopping list.'

'Do they ever go their own ways? They're not identical twins, are they?'

154

'No, they're not. They could be, if they were t'same size, but little Rene's the quiet one and she often goes off alone, showing her sheep.'

'I get the impression they're hard working,' I commented. 'Salt of the earth and all that.'

'They've no need to work, Mr Rhea. That father of theirs left 'em thousands. Did you get into their living-room?'

I shook my head.

'You're not an artist, are you?' he appeared to change the subject and I shook my head again.

'But you'll have heard of Reynolds, have you?'

'The portrait painter?' I asked. 'Sir Joshua Reynolds?'

'Aye, that's him. Well, they've five or six Reynolds paintings in that house, and antique furniture too, silver, jewellery ...'

'Up there?' I cried. 'In that old farmhouse?'

He nodded solemnly. 'They're loaded, Mr Rhea. They've no need to work, but they stick it out there in the hills, working themselves hard day and night.'

He prattled on about their inherited wealth and their total ignorance of its capacity to give them an easy life, and then said, 'I reckon they ought to have burglar alarms fitted, Mr Rhea. That's why I thought I'd mention it. If somebody broke in and took those pictures alone, they'd lose thousands ...'

'I'll pop in and see them next week,' I promised.

'And look out for their latest man,' he waved a finger at me.

'Latest man?' I asked, smiling at him.

A broad grin flitted across his face and he ran his hand across his bald head. 'Aye,' he laughed. 'They've had a succession of men working for them, year in and year out.'

'Doing what?' I asked.

'Tending sheep or pigs, and general labouring,' he told me. 'Heavy work, mainly, but some skilled fellers have been through their hands. They never stay long.'

'Don't they? Why?' I asked in all innocence.

'They fall in love with the fellow,' he laughed. 'Cis and Rene each fall in love with the poor devil at the same time. It always happens – within five or six months of the new bloke being there, they both start falling for him. Then there's jealousy, and Rene has a go at Cis's pigs and Cis has a go at Rene's sheep, and if it coincides with a show date somewhere, there's hell on …'

'And?'

'The poor chap is driven out. I've lost count of their fellers,' he laughed. 'Every poor sod finds himself fighting their battles and protecting their animals against the other's vicious attacks … then they both blame him for falling in love with the other and for sticking up for the other's animals.'

'Does it ever reach my official ears?' I asked, visualising domestic turmoil out at Slape Wath Farm.

'No, it rarely gets out – they seldom go anywhere, and the fellers come and go quietly.'

But I did get involved with them and their current love affair with Jack Holtby. I saw him for the first time when I went along to discuss the treasures in their house. He was having his 'lowance and I was invited to join them at the kitchen table, where I tucked into a meal large enough for the average man's lunch.

He was a dark-haired man in his fifties, with a heavily scarred face which was apparently the result of being trapped in a tank during the war. A small man, he was wiry and sparsely built, but had a ready smile for me as I joined him at the table. He was dressed neatly, albeit in working clothes, and appeared to be slightly on the shy side. As I talked to the ladies, he made an excuse and left, saying he was just popping up to his room before returning to work.

Two pairs of blue eyes followed his progress and I could see the signs of unrequited love. I wondered what problems it would bring to him.

But I was here to talk about security.

After my scones and coffee, I broached the subject of the paintings and the ladies agreed they were valuable, although neither had any idea of the total worth of their treasures. Neither had I, for I lay no claim to knowledge of antiques or works of art, but when I saw the array of Reynoldses and other valuables, I knew that this house was a veritable museum, a treasure trove of remarkable interest.

Following my visit to the downstairs rooms, they showed me around the upper floor, including all six bedrooms and the attic of their rambling old home. Every room was richly endowed with solid antique furniture and I noticed lots of pictures, large and small, but all of considerable age.

All about the house was the smell of age and dampness, except in Jack's bedroom where I discerned a different aroma. I could not identify the scent, but it was not pipe smoke and not old socks or sweaty feet. I dismissed the question as I continued to survey the house and its contents.

Downstairs, I told the curious pair that I intended to call in the Crime Prevention Officer from our Divisional Headquarters, and he would undertake a professional survey of the house, free of charge, with a view to recommending some form of protection. I also advised them to consult Norman Taylor with a possibility of taking out some insurance. While discussing the protection of their inheritance, I did worry somewhat about the presence of Jack Holtby, for I knew nothing of his past or of his character.

My first impressions were that he was an average farm worker who would never appreciate the wealth of treasures around him, and I felt they were secure in his presence. He would not talk about them because he would not recognise them for what they were, but there is a breed of villain who preys on innocent or elderly people. These are like ravenous wolves, pitiless and cruel, for they rob their elders and their descendants of their rightful inheritance. It was such scoundrels from whom the Misses Kirby must be protected, and that was my duty.

I could not ignore the presence of their 'latest man' however, and resolved to keep a watchful eye upon him and his contacts. I'd check his background too. Meanwhile, the official wheels could be set in motion, and our Crime Prevention Officer would be told.

Some weeks later, the survey was complete, and a recommended burglar alarm company arrived to fit their clever device. I was not there during these operations, although we did note the car numbers and the names of the workmen just in case they turned out to be less than honest. However, the deed was completed and the Misses Kirby were fully equipped with a modern and highly sophisticated burglar alarm.

To set it, there was a box of tricks on the wall at the foot of the stairs, and after locking the doors and windows, the box itself was activated by locking it with a key. That key was then removed and stored in a secure place. Upon leaving the house, the key was also removed and the outer door was locked, thus sealing the system. After this, any severance of a contact, either by opening a door or window, would cause loud bells to ring at the farm and a little light to flash in our Divisional Headquarters. At last, the Kirby treasures were in care.

The system was fine, moderately expensive and highly efficient. But it lacked one important factor. It did not contain the brain of a woman, and furthermore, it could not cope with the female habit of losing keys. Women the world over lock themselves out of houses, offices and cars, and it means that a burglar alarm in any female environment is something of a hazard.

Frances and Rene were no exception. They lost innumerable keys of their alarm system. The angry machine rang bells across the moors and flashed lights in the police station; it summoned countless frustrated technicians to the remote farm to reset the device and to supply them with a new key. In time, everyone involved – police, crime prevention officers, the insurance and the burglar alarm company – lost count of the number of times they attended these false alarms and reset the system. The ladies could not learn to safeguard the precious and all-important key.

Eventually, the insurance company put its foot down. Norman had the job of telling the ladies that his company would not accept further liability for the contents of their home because the ladies themselves were a bigger risk. Norman talked to me about it, and I talked to our Crime Prevention Officer; together we studied a long missive from the insurance company.

The problem was all to do with lost keys. The insurance company was not at all happy about the security of the key for the lock which was the nerve centre for the entire system. The company was even more upset when one of their inspectors called unexpectedly and found the key left in the lock, with a long piece of string reaching from the key to a nail in the wall. It seemed they'd decided to keep the key there, where everyone could use it and from where it would never stray. If it remained on that piece of string, it would never get lost.

The insurance man was not at all happy with that system. There were long discussions with the ladies, and then Frances chanced to mention their safes. It seemed each lady had a safe built into the wall of her bedroom, tucked well away behind the bed. These contained personal cash and private things, and were used for their trophies, for cups and medals won at agricultural shows. Each safe was operated by a numerical code known only to the owner. If each kept a key for the burglar alarm in her own safe, the problem might be solved. It would mean the introduction of a new rule for the company, i.e. two keys for this one alarm, but by issuing each with a key, the system might function correctly.

Norman put this to his company and they agreed. After inspecting each safe and studying their individual security systems, which were designed to prevent one another from snooping, the insurance company agreed to continue the ladies on risk. I was happy too, and for a while there were no more ringing bells, flashing lights and emergency calls from Slape Wath Farm. Each lady kept her personal key secure in her own safe and they learned to use these to set the alarm each night upon retiring, and each time they vacated the farm.

Peace reigned, and the treasures were protected.

It would be several weeks later when I received a

sad telephone call from Frances Kirby. She rang about ten thirty one Friday morning, and just caught me before I vanished into my hilly beat.

'Mr Rhea,' she burbled into the telephone. 'You've got to come, it's Jack.'

'Jack?' For a moment I'd forgotten about their live-in handyman.

'You know, Jack that works for us.'

'Oh, that Jack! What's happened?'

For one horrible moment, I thought he must have absconded with their best silver, antiques and money, but she was speaking gently and with some feeling. Her voice was about to crack and I wondered what awful thing had happened to Jack. I thought of accidents, sudden death, electrocution, drowning, maiming by cows ... all sorts of ghastly occurrences flashed through my mind.

'He's gone, Mr Rhea. He's gone and left us. It's our Rene's fault, the silly bitch ... she won't leave him alone. I've told her and told her again and again, but she's been chasing him like a love-sick virgin ...'

She prattled on about Jack's absence and I found myself suppressing a smile. I remembered what Joe Steel had told me about them driving away their menfolk and guessed this was just another in a long line of absconding lovers. Jack must have grown heartily sick of coping with two of them.

'How old is he?' I interrupted her chatter.

'Fifty-two,' she said without hesitating.

'Then there's nothing I can do,' I began to tell her. 'If a grown man wishes to leave home or his place of employment, it is not a matter for the police ...'

'Ah'm worried,' she cried. 'Mr Rhea, Ah'm so worried. It's not a bit like him, not like him at all, and

161

Ah think he might have come to some harm. Oh dear, Ah wish that silly sister o' mine would lay off … he'll never marry her, Ah could see it in his eyes. He wasn't in love with her, Mr Rhea, not Jack. It was me, really, thoo knows, Ah was t'one he favoured …'

'Look, Cis,' I said. 'Shall I come up to see you? Maybe he's just gone off for the day?'

'No, he's gone for ever. He's locked his bedroom door and bolted. Gone.'

It happened that I was about due to visit Slape Wath Farm for a routine stock check and I decided to pop in today. After all, I could make a cursory search of the premises, just in case poor old Jack had got his head fast in some machinery or fallen into a midden. It would show interest from me.

I shouted through to Mary that I had changed my intended destination and would not be back for lunch. One of the farmers in those moors would feed me before nightfall, I was sure. I was just heading out of my little office when the telephone rang again. I was tempted to ignore it, but realised it might be something more urgent than Frances's missing man.

'Aidensfield Police, PC Rhea,' I announced myself.

'Mr Rhea? This is Rene Kirby. You must come at once.'

'What's the matter, Rene?' I wondered if Cis had now fallen into the midden or got her head fast in a pig trough.

'Jack,' she said with tears in her voice, 'He's gone, Mr Rhea.'

'Yes, I know. Frances rang a few minutes ago. I'm coming up to see if I can help.'

'Rang? She rang? The scheming bitch! She's driven him away, Mr Rhea, so she has. All that courting and lovey-dovey slop she's been dishing out to him. She's after him, Mr Rhea, she won't leave the fellow alone, poor sod. Double rations of apple pie, more custard than a fellow can cope with, best crockery at tea-time – name it, she's done it for him.'

'Has she?' I was astounded by this revelation. What more could a fellow want if he was getting double rations of custard?

The more she ranted about her sister, the more I appreciated the words of our village shopkeeper. Now I knew what life was all about at Slape Wath Farm.

I had no idea how many men the quaint pair had driven away, but I did appreciate that Jack was just one of a long, long line. I would go to the farm to express my sorrow and show interest in their dilemma, then maybe if I talked about agricultural shows and prize-winning pigs or sheep, I'd get them to forget the departed Jack.

But it didn't work. When I arrived at the farm, I found them both in the kitchen, sitting at opposite sides of the table with a pot of tea between them and three mugs awaiting. Big Cis saw me first and came to greet me, her eyes red with crying. Rene also sported two red-rimmed eyes, and sniffed into a lace handkerchief.

'Mr Rhea, oh, Mr Rhea, Ah'm so glad you've come...'

Rene added, 'because we've not seen him for hours and hours and there's been no call, no letter ... and it's not like Jack ...'

'He would have said something, you know, left a note for me ...'

'For me, you silly bitch, for me.'

'Ladies, ladies!' I cried, settling down at the table. 'All this bickering will do no good. Now you both love

163

him?'

I was relying on Joe Steel's past assessment to deal with this situation.

There was a long silence, then Cis nodded.

'Yes, he was such a nice, kind man …'

'And so good to the animals, Mr Rhea. The way he handled a …'

'Pig or a sheep was magic to watch. Superb, he was, Mr Rhea, a real man …'

'And a friend, Mr Rhea, a real friend.'

I listened to this double-sided conversation, and remembered what Frances had said when ringing me this morning.

'Frances,' I said, 'you told me he'd locked his bedroom door and bolted?'

She nodded fiercely.

'She's driven him away, Mr Rhea,' butted in Rene. 'He's cleared off, never to return. Every time Ah find myself a nice man-friend, she gets her claws into him and frightens him off …'

'She frightens him off, not me. Throwing herself at him like that … baking cakes for his birthday, I ask you! And sending Valentine cards!'

'Hang on, hang on!' I shouted above their banter. 'Look,' I raised my voice and caught their attention, 'did you set your burglar alarm last night?'

My change of tactic surprised them and both regarded me with puzzled expressions.

'Burglar alarm, Mr Rhea?' asked Rene.

'You mean our alarm, Mr Rhea?' followed Cis.

By this time, I was heading towards the control-box of their system and saw the familiar key in the lock, with a length of string dangling from it. A cotton reel hung on the end.

'Ah!' I said, spotting this. 'This should not be here, should it?'

'It was awkward, going upstairs to our safes, Mr Rhea ...'

'We kept forgetting and t'alarm kept going off, and so we hid a key in t'knife drawer ... that's t'one, t'key we all use, us and Jack that is, it's t'only one left ...'

'If Norman's insurance company saw this, they'd never cover you again, you know. There's no point in having a burglar alarm if you leave the key in all the time ...'

'Nobody's going to burgle us, Mr Rhea, nobody ...'

'Our geese and dogs will stop 'em, Mr Rhea ...'

Then I guessed where Jack was.

'Look,' I said, 'when you go to bed, you turn the key and set your alarm. Is that right?'

'Yes, Mr Rhea, we do that,' they both spoke at once.

'And you leave the key in?'

'No, we put it in the knife drawer, so we both know where it is.'

'Would Jack know where it is?' I put to them.

'No, he thinks we put the keys in the safes, because that's what we told the insurance man,' again they spoke together.

'So if Jack had come downstairs last night and crept away, he'd have set off the alarm, wouldn't he?'

Cis nodded and so did Rene.

'Yes, Mr Rhea.'

'Yes, Mr Rhea.'

'But he didn't set it off, and Cis said his bedroom door was locked, so that means he's still in the room, doesn't it?'

As I said it, I visualised him lying dead on his bed,

having suffered a massive heart attack during the night. I'd dealt with many sudden deaths of this kind and this sounded like another. It looked as if I was going to be busy.

They were already galloping upstairs, their voices shrill and harsh as they careered towards the bedroom of the object they worshipped so dearly. Both were hammering on the door as I reached it, panting slightly from the steep climb.

They stood aside, gabbling incessantly and wiping their flooding eyes as I stepped forward and turned the knob. Nothing. It was locked and I guessed the key was on the inside. I knocked many times and shouted loudly.

'Jack? Are you there?'

There was nothing, not even a groan of pain or a half-hearted attempt to reply. I looked at my watch. Eleven thirty. And as I hammered on the door and shouted, I could faintly discern the peculiar smell I'd noticed previously when looking around the rooms. Now, I thought I knew what it was. If I was right, Jack wasn't dead.

'Well?' they both asked at once, expecting me to perform a miracle.

'Have you a ladder?' I asked.

'Ladder?' they chorused. 'What for?'

'To look into his room,' I said seriously. 'I think he's in there and I think I know what's the matter.'

'He's there?' they shouted. 'You mean he hasn't left us?'

'I'll have to see.' I didn't promise anything, but we all trooped downstairs and out into the foldyard. There hanging on a wall inside a shed was a long ladder, and I carried this to his bedroom window. Propping it carefully against the wall, I began my climb of exploration.

As I reached the bottom pane, I peered inside and knew my diagnosis had been correct. I could see Jack laid on the cover of his untidy, unmade bed, and he was out like the proverbial light. His head lay on the pillow and his mouth was wide open, an invitation to flies and passing spiders, while his hands lay palm upwards at the end of outspread arms. His feet, bare and black, hung over the end of the bed, and he was dressed in blue striped pyjamas. He was not a pretty sight.

From my position on the ladder, I could peer right into the room, and saw evidence of my suspicions. That smell had been alcohol, gallons and gallons of it, the sort that reeks when poured down human throats without ceasing, year after year, and which fills rooms like this when empty bottles are left around. Jack Holtby was an alcoholic. Even from this distance, the room bore the classic signs. There were bottles everywhere. Stout, beer, spirits, full ones and empties, all littered about the place, filling every spare inch of space. The window ledge, the mantelpiece, the top of the wardrobe, the drawers, the dressing-table – all were full of bottles, standing or lying, empty and full, and the floor was similarly littered. The fellow was as drunk as a newt.

I opened the window in the manner used by enterprising burglars and clambered inside, knocking bottles aside. The stench was appalling. Holding my breath, I raised the window to its full height to allow some fresh air inside, and noticed the two anxious faces below.

'I'm checking,' I yelled at them. 'He's here.'

'Oh!' they cried, putting their hands to their mouths.

'Is he ill?'

'I think so,' I deigned to answer, and picked my way through the minefield of bottles towards the bed. I felt him; he was warm. He was therefore alive and I could just hear his faint breathing. I slapped his cheeks, but got no response. He was out cold, stoned out of his mind and I wondered if the ladies had driven him to drink …

Probably not. Probably, he was well on the way to alcoholic oblivion before getting this job, and this made it easy for him to avoid prying eyes. To be tucked away out here with two doting spinsters must have been a gift from the gods. No wonder he'd kept himself to himself.

I unlocked the door with the key left in the lock and made my way downstairs. They were hurrying towards me with worried expressions.

'Is he ill?'

'Or dead? Fallen and hurt himself?'

'Has he ever asked either of you for drinks?' I put to them.

'Yes,' each said in perfect unison, 'but he told me not to tell my sister. I got him drink from the village when I went down …'

'As a secret? A special favour because you loved him … ?' I smiled.

They didn't answer. Each was blushing, each had been skilfully used by this chronic alcoholic and each had served only to keep him well stocked up with booze of every conceivable kind. And last night, he'd reduced his stock by a fair margin.

'He's drunk,' I said. 'He's out like a light, totally and finally sloshed. He's an alcoholic, ladies, the room is full of bottles.'

They looked at each other and didn't speak.

168

'I'll call the doctor,' I said. 'I think he needs medical attention of some kind. Can I use your telephone?'

'Of course, Mr Rhea.'

When I called again three months later, Jack had gone. They introduced me to another man, a grey-haired slim man in his fifties. He sat with them at their kitchen table, sipping coffee and I saw the familiar light in their eyes.

'This is Ernest Wallace,' beamed Cis. 'He's been with us a few weeks ...'

'He came from Waversford Estate, Mr Rhea, with very good references ...'

'I know he'll be well looked after,' I smiled, pulling up a chair. 'Welcome, Mr Wallace.'

I made a mental note to check his character and I wondered how he'd cope with a moorland burglar alarm and two love-sick spinsters.

Chapter 8

'In works of labour, or of skill,
I would be busy too;
For Satan finds some mischief still
For idle hands to do.'

ISAAC WATTS (1674–1748)

BECAUSE IT WAS SATURDAY, the grandfather clock had to be wound up. I opened the ancient glass door which covered the face and reached to the top of the case for the key. I kept it there because it was out of reach of the children and I knew where to find it each winding day. The key was a curious shape, being a tiny tunnel with a handle welded at one end, and it was used to wind the eight-day clock. It looked something like a miniature starting handle for a car.

As I wound up the faithful old clock, the key suddenly broke in my hand. The delicate handle had come away from the barrel of the antique key, and I could see it was nothing more than a straightforward welding job. The repair could be quickly affected.

At first, I thought of Awd John the blacksmith, but on second thoughts appreciated that his skills were more directed towards the repair of larger objects like ploughs and gates. I had never seen him tackle anything of a delicate nature, and I wondered if anyone in this village could fix my key. It was more than a soldering job, I realised, otherwise I would have done that myself. Welding was the only sure way of effecting this repair. The garage might have done it, but they closed on Saturday afternoons.

Accordingly, I decided to ask around the village, and the first man I saw as I patrolled on foot about the village centre was Stumpy Sykes.

'Now, Stumpy,' I made the traditional greeting. 'How's tha gahin on?'

'Middling,' was his reply. Everything Stumpy did was middling – never good, never bad. If he was ill, he was middling; if he was fit and well, he was middling. If he won a prize in the flower shows, his plants were fair to middling, and whatever the weather, it was middling.

'Stumpy,' I said, taking the broken key from my pocket. 'Is there anybody who can fix this?'

He solemnly regarded the key and nodded slowly. 'Deearn't trust Awd John wi summat like that. Welding ploughs and fixing rainwater pipes is right up his street, but fixing delicate things like yon is not in his line at all. Try Awd Alex.'

'Alex?' I puzzled.

'Aye, that cottage yon side o' t'garage. He's a retired clock-maker, well into his seventies, but he can fix owt.'

I'd not come across Awd Alex and learned his surname was MacDonald. Mr Alexander MacDonald to be precise, and he lived with his wife in a lovely cottage with a porch and climbing plants all over the front. The place shone like a polished cream-strainer. I knocked on the door, using a brass knocker in which I could see my own reflection, and soon a smart lady in her sixties answered. Her pretty face expressed surprise

171

at the sight of my uniform but she rapidly gained her composure and said, 'Yes?'

'Oh, I'm PC Rhea,' I introduced myself. 'I'm looking for Mr MacDonald.'

'Oh, nothing's wrong, is it?' she asked the question everyone asked when finding a policeman at the door. I noticed she carried a yellow duster.

'Oh, no,' I smiled and pulled the key from my pocket. 'It's this – I'm told he can fix it.'

'Well, yes, I suppose he can, Officer.' She spoke with a faint Scots accent. 'But he's out just now. You can find him up at Miss Crowther's – you know her place?'

I shook my head.

'Stone House,' she said, pointing along the village. 'You could leave the thing if you want – he's got a workshop up the garden.'

'No, I'll explain how it needs fixing,' I smiled. 'I'll find him. Miss Crowther, eh?'

'Yes, he went there a long time ago – I hope you find him – if you do, Officer, can you say tea will be ready at five o'clock?'

'Yes, of course,' and I left her to her cleaning.

I walked along the main street, bidding 'Good afternoon' to several residents and finally reached Stone House, Miss Crowther's home. It was a large, Victorian building of sombre grey stone and boasted a rather genteel but unkempt appearance. I had to lift the garden gate to open it, for it needed new hinges, and made my way to the front door. I rang the bell and it sounded somewhere inside, upon which I eventually heard inner doors opening and closing as someone came towards me. Then the front door opened.

A short, dumpy and smiling woman answered; she

was clad in a long purple dress with a knitted shawl over the shoulders and smiled a warm welcome.

'Ah,' she said, 'You must be Police Constable Rhea?'

'Yes,' I acknowledged.

'It's so kind of you to call,' she oozed, 'I'm delighted you have found the time. I do like the policemen to call on me, to make themselves known so that when I'm in trouble, I know who they are. That makes it so much easier to approach you, and it gives us all that much more confidence …'

As she ushered me inside her rambling home, she babbled on and guided me into a large lounge expensively furnished with Indian carpets and complementary furnishings. She motioned me to sit down and I obeyed.

'Now,' she said. 'Tea or coffee?'

'Well, actually,' I began, 'I didn't come to stay …'

'Nonsense, you can't call without some hospitality in return,' she breathed. 'I do like to give my policemen a drink or two. Biscuits?'

And before I could answer, she whisked away towards her pantry somewhere along the corridor and returned with a plate full of chocolate biscuits. She placed these on a low table, which she eased towards me and said, 'Tea won't be a jiffy.'

At that, she settled on the chair opposite and began to ask about my family. I happily obliged, occasionally trying to explain the real purpose of my visit, but it was quite plain she'd interpreted this as a purely social call, a 'get-to-know-you' exercise. So I played along with this, knowing it would please her. She told me of her father, a senior army officer in India years ago, and of her brothers who were very clever and doing well in

173

London, one a barrister and the other in exports of some kind. She spent well over forty minutes telling me all about herself and asking all about me. She was a charming lady, most articulate and well read, and I knew I was going to have difficulty getting away. Furthermore, I had to find out where Mr MacDonald had gone – perhaps he was still in the house?

I managed to include his name in the conversation as I found myself telling her the names of those people with whom I'd made contact in the short time I'd been here. When I mentioned Alex MacDonald, she said, 'Oh, nice man. Very nice man. I had him in here before you came. He came to fix my television set, it was doing funny things. He's good at fixing things, is Mr MacDonald, very good.'

'I'd like to meet him,' I said, thinking of the broken clock key in my pocket.

'He said he was going down to old Mr Nash's house,' she said.

'I'll see him later,' I said. 'It wasn't important.'

'Well, I mustn't keep you,' she beamed. 'It was so kind of you to call. Do call again, anytime you like, and we'll have tea.'

And so I walked into the fresh air, rather baffled by her warm reception, but determined to call again and hear more of her fascinating life.

I knew Mr Nash. He was an old gentleman who had retired from a life in the city, something to do with accountancy, and I often chattered to him in the street, or in the shop. I knew he would welcome me, and that he was a kindred spirit of Alex MacDonald. I found his neat semi tucked well into the corner of a new estate, and walked up the path. He was gardening and observed my approach.

He raised a soil-stained hand in greeting as I strode along his path.

'Hello, Mr Nash. Still tidying up then?'

'There's always work in a garden,' he said, leaning on his rake. 'But it keeps me busy. My wife has gone into York, looking for a new dress, so I pretended I had this patch to get raked over urgently ...' and he grinned wickedly at his private conspiracy.

'I'm looking for Alex MacDonald,' I said. 'I heard he was here.'

'Yes, he was. I got him to fix the overflow in my roof. The confounded thing keeps overflowing every time we have a bath, and as he's such a good plumber, I thought he'd fix it. He hasn't been gone long.'

'Where did he go?' I asked.

'Up to Joe Steel's.'

That meant the village shop.

By this stage, I was most interested in Awd Alex, as Stumpy had called him. I'd been sent to him because he was a useful welder, but already this afternoon he'd fixed Miss Crowther's television set and Mr Nash's plumbing. Why had he gone to the shop – it was closed on Saturday afternoons?

'How long since?' I asked him.

'Not long – maybe an hour, no more.'

I was determined to track down the elusive Alex MacDonald, and after passing the time of day with Mr Nash and admiring his garden, I walked back up the village to the shop. Although it was shut, I knew Joe Steel would respond to my knocking. He did, and seemed pleased to see me.

'Hello, Mr Rhea. Trouble?'

'No trouble,' I smiled. 'Sorry to bother you, Joe, but I'm looking for Alex MacDonald.'

'Oh, he's gone,' he told me. 'I had him here not long ago – an hour ago, not much more. He does a spot of wine tasting for me, you know. I get wine in for my customers and he tastes samples for me – he knows a bit about his wines, he's very good with German whites…'

'Where did he go from here?' I heard myself ask patiently.

'Mrs Widdowson,' he said. 'She's having trouble with her lights. They keep going out – there's a bad connection, I think, or a short somewhere. Bulbs keep blowing or the lights keep flickering. He's gone round there to fix them for her.'

'Thanks – I'll see if he's there.'

'He left about forty minutes ago,' he said.

I knew I was getting warmer. The time-lapse was growing less and less as I pursued the elusive Alex around the village. Joe told me how to find Mrs Widdowson and I located her in a lovely bungalow just off the main street. She was washing her windows from a short step-ladder and would be a lady in her early fifties. She wore a flowered head-square and flat shoes.

'Hello,' I shouted across to her. 'Mrs Widdowson?'

'Yes,' she returned my smile with that inevitable look of apprehension.

'I'm looking for Mr MacDonald,' I announced. 'I was told he was here.'

'Yes, he was, Mr Rhea,' she knew my name. 'He came to fix my lights – it was a bad connection, he said. He fixed it for me. He left, though, about half an hour ago. He doesn't take long, fixing things.'

'He doesn't!' I said. 'Thanks – sorry to have troubled you.'

'He said he was going over to Partridge Hall,' she

176

offered. 'You know, that farm down the Elsinby Road.'

'I know,' I called, deciding to complete this tour. I had to visit the Dinsdale family at Partridge Hall sometime in the near future, to interview Terry, their seventeen-year-old son. He'd been involved in a motorcycle accident near Manchester last week, so I could conclude these two missions together. The walk to Partridge Hall took about twenty minutes. I walked towards the spacious entrance of this lovely old building which was really a large farmhouse set among sycamores. It stood on an elevated site with ranging views across the open countryside and was clearly the home of an industrious and wealthy family.

I rang the doorbell and waited. Soon, a young woman with neat blonde hair tied with a ribbon appeared from a corridor and smiled at me.

'Hello,' I said. 'I'm PC Rhea. Is Terry Dinsdale in please?'

'Terry?' she frowned. 'Is he in trouble?'

'No,' I assured her. 'It's about his accident last week, the one near Manchester. I've got to take a statement from him – it's for the local police. I think he was more of a witness than a casualty?'

'Yes, he was overtaken by a motor-cyclist who crashed into a van. Terry fell off his motorbike because of it, but wasn't hurt. I think he's out. Just a moment, I'll fetch mum.'

She disappeared the way she had come and soon a mature woman with identical blonde hair and lovely smile materialised from the house. She was dressed in painting clothes – an old apron, old dress and a clear plastic hat on her head. She carried a paint brush, the handle wrapped in a rag.

'Oh, I'm sorry,' I said. 'I didn't want to interrupt

important work!'

'It's all right, I'm decorating our lounge,' she said. 'Susan said it's Terry you want?'

I explained the reason and she smiled. 'Yes, he told us, but he's out, Mr Rhea. He went off to York with some pals. I expect him back about half past six.'

'I'll call again.'

'Shall I send him up to your house?' she offered.

'If he rings first to tell me when he's coming, that would be fine,' I consented.

'He won't be prosecuted, will he?' she asked, with all the worried expressions a mother can produce.

'Not from what I saw of the report from Manchester,' I confirmed. 'I've been asked to take a witness statement from him, nothing more, although I will have to record details of his driving licence and insurance. That's routine.'

'All right, Mr Rhea, I'll get him to ring you when he comes in.'

'Thanks – now, a small thing while I'm here. I'm looking for Mr MacDonald and understand he's here.'

'Yes,' she smiled, and I felt a great sense of relief. 'Did you want to speak to him?'

'Very briefly,' and I pulled my key from my pocket. 'I want him to fix this, and have been chasing him all afternoon.'

'Come through,' she invited, and I followed her along the elegant corridors of this beautiful old house and into a room which reeked of fresh paint. The floor and furniture were covered with white sheets and there, perched high on a step ladder, was a silver-haired gentleman with a deeply tanned face. He was the picture of health and he turned to look down as I entered the room. He was clad in a white smock and put something down on the tray at the top of his ladder. Above was a highly ornate ceiling, rich in plaster work and decorated across its entirety. He was doing something to the plaster work.

'Mr MacDonald,' the lady announced. 'This is PC Rhea, he wants a quick word with you.'

'Guilty as charged!' he raised his hands in the air and laughed, then descended the tall step-ladder. 'Hello, I'm Alex MacDonald.' His voice had a pleasing lowland lilt.

I showed him the key and he smiled. 'No problem,' he said. 'Is it from a gramophone or a clock?'

'A grandfather clock,' I said.

'I'll fix it next week. Will you be at home on Wednesday morning?'

I made a rapid mental calculation, and said, 'Yes, I'll be in my office until ten o'clock, at the Hill Top. But I can call in at your place.' He took my key and popped it into his pocket.

'I take a lot of catching,' he smiled. 'Wednesday is my day at Ashfordly – I go to the bread shop, you know and bake their fruit cakes for them. I can drop your key in as I pass the house.'

'That's fine,' I said. 'Really fine …'

My business over, I left the room and Mrs Dinsdale escorted me to the front door. 'He's remarkable,' she was saying. 'He's putting gold leaf on to my ceiling, making a marvellous job too. We only decorate that ceiling once every fifteen years or so, and it's a job finding someone who can do that gold leaf work. I was lucky getting Mr MacDonald.'

'Yes, you were,' I agreed. I reached the door, and as I was about to leave, I heard footsteps behind me. Alex MacDonald was hurrying after me.

'Oh, Mr Rhea,' he panted. 'If that grandfather clock of yours grows awkward, you know where to find me. I'll fix it for you – reset the timing, weights, and so forth.'

'Thanks,' I smiled, as I left the premises. I wondered if he was any good at working night duty for bored policemen!

Ted Williamson from Keld House rang me at seven one morning and cried, 'Mr Rhea, thoo'll etti come quick. Ah've had some sheep pinched during t'night.'

I didn't ask any more questions, but donned my motorcycling gear and set out across the hills to his remote farm. It lay at the end of a deep, narrow valley high on the moors, and was extremely isolated. His sheep ran across the moors with no hedges or walls to contain them and they formed a major contribution to his meagre living standards. He did, however, keep a few sheep closer to the house and these were in a small paddock adjacent to the building. These had been bred by hand by his patient wife, the lambs of mothers who had either rejected them or who had died during lambing time. Those orphans had grown into fine animals, thanks to her attention.

The noise of my arrival brought him from the kitchen and he was waiting on the concrete path as I struggled to park my bike upon an irregular and stony farmyard. At last I had the machine balanced on its stand, and removed my crash helmet which I placed on the seat.

'Morning, Ted,' I greeted him. 'Sad affair, eh?'

'Aye, lad, it is. Now, them sheep o' mine roam across yon heights with nivver a theft from one year end to t'next; some get knocked down and killed by cars, but thoo can expect that. Sheep aren't t'brightest o' creatures, are they?'

'No, they're a bit dim,' I agreed, following him to the kitchen.

'But them in that paddock, well, they've been hand-reared by our Maud and some is as tame as a cat. Some rotten sod has pinched 'em from that paddock.'

'How many?' I put to him as I pulled a chair from the table. It scraped noisily upon the sandstone floor, and I sat down without being asked. It was expected that visitors did this.

'Eight,' he said. 'Eight gimmers, nice animals, well fed. Nice for meat, Ah'd say, plump and fleshy. Not run to bone like them awd ewes up on t'top. Some butcher'll have 'em by now, Ah reckon, cutting 'em up.'

'Morning, Mr Rhea,' Maud, his plump, rosy-cheeked wife came in with a large metal teapot and said. 'Tea?'

'Thanks.' She began to pour a huge tin mug full, a pint pot with a metal handle.

'What are they worth, Ted?' I had to ask for my crime report.

'Fifteen quid apiece, Ah reckon.'

I sipped the tea and they settled before me, sitting around the table as I produced a long sheet of paper from my inside pocket. This was a crime report, and I had to enter all the relevant details upon it. I began with the standard questions about their names, ages, addresses and occupations, and eventually got down to the basic facts of the crime. From what Ted told me, he'd checked the paddock last night about ten o'clock before turning in to bed, and at quarter to seven this morning, he'd come downstairs to find the gate open. He knew he'd locked it last night – he'd checked that very fact before going to bed.

About a dozen sheep were still in the field, huddled in a corner, and he believed they'd been terrified into moving there in the dark, and had not strayed since.

'Could it be hikers?' I asked. 'Maybe somebody's walked through and just left the gate open? Could your sheep have wandered off?'

He shook his head vigorously. 'Nay, lad, nivver. If that had happened, they'd still be on my land somewhere. They're not – they've been takken off in a truck of some kind.'

'Truck?'

'Van mebbe. Summat light, I reckon, like a pick-up or a small van.'

'How do you know that?'

'There's tracks in that gateway. Drink your tea, and Ah'll show you.'

Meanwhile, I wrote into my report a description of the eight missing gimmers, the name used for young female sheep not yet ewes. All were nine months old, female of course, and marked on their left flank with a splotch of blue dye. After completing those short but essential formalities, I asked Ted to take me to the scene of the crime.

'That gate,' he said.

And in the soft earth were the unmistakable tracks of a vehicle of some kind. It had reversed into the gateway, a fact revealed by marks of its front wheels made during that manoeuvre, and there was a slight indentation a few feet into the field where a long tailboard or ramp had rested. I knew how the thief had operated – in the darkness, he would park his vehicle in the open gate and simply drive the sheep towards the truck. There may have been a dog, and he must have had lights of some kind, but it was a simple manoeuvre. Once he'd got a handful of animals aboard, he would drive off.

I squatted on my haunches to examine the marks. They were the conventional tyre marks of a four-wheeled light vehicle, and I guessed it was a pick-up of some kind, possibly a Morris. Then I noticed the irregularity in one of the rear tyre marks.

From the impressions in the soft earth, it was clear that the tyre had a defect on the inside wall, and it looked like a bubble of rubber. I knew the fault – it had once happened to my car. The tyre wall was weak and the pressure of air caused the tube and the tyre to bulge like a round bubble. If it caught a sharp stone or a nail, a puncture was inevitable. Sometimes, if the blob grew very large, it would make contact with the springs of the vehicle and create a nuisance, if only because of the repetitious noise as the wheel turned. But in time, that would rub a hole in the outer casing.

I showed this to Ted.

'Now that's a capper,' he said. 'Ah nivver noticed yon.'

'Does it ring a bell?' I asked. 'Has anybody been up here lately with a vehicle like this? I reckon it's a small pick-up, four wheels, all single and with a tail-board that comes down, like a ramp.'

'And with a blob on t'rear tyre, eh? On t'inside?'

'You can see the mark in the soil, Ted.' I pointed to it again, and I could see he was thinking hard.

'Noo, there was a feller up here with a truck like that, seeking work.'

'When was this?' I began to grow excited.

'Two days back, no more.'

'What did he want?'

'He came to my kitchen door one afternoon, three o'clock or thereabouts, and asked if Ah was looking for casual labour.'

'Did you take him on, Ted?'

He shook his head, 'Nay, lad. Ah've a spot of ditching and hedging that mebbe needs a feller to do it, but Ah didn't want to take onnybody on. To be honest, Ah can't afford to pay for jobs like that.'

'So he left?'

'Aye, he did.'

'And who was it? A local?'

'Ah didn't ask his name, Mr Rhea. But he gave some name or other. Daft of me when Ah think back, but Ah didn't write it down. You don't think at the time, do you? Ah've seen him around at market days and sheep sales, mind.'

'What's he look like?' I was taking notes now.

'A little feller, with a sharp face, like a jockey or even an elf! A funny little chap, really. Scruffily dressed, mind.'

Immediately, I knew my suspect. I said, 'And was his van a light blue one, with rust all over? A Morris pick-up, like we thought?'

He frowned and then nodded. 'Aye, now you come to mention it, it was.'

'Can you remember his name? Try hard.'

He shrugged his shoulders. 'It didn't ring a bell, I can't remember it.'

'Claude Jeremiah Greengrass?' I suggested.

'Aye!' his eyes lit up. 'That was what he said. A daft sooart of a name if you ask me … thoo knows him?'

'I know him,' I agreed. 'He's a petty thief who lives on my patch near Elsinby. This is just the sort of thing he'd do.'

184

'If you catch him, will it mean court then?'

'You bet it will!' I said. 'I've been after this rogue for ages, Ted, and he always manages to get away somehow.'

'Well, Ah's nut one for takking folks to court, Mr Rhea, nut if I can help it. All Ah want is them sheep back, that's all.'

If I knew Claude Jeremiah, he'd have disposed of the animals very rapidly, thus getting rid of the evidence. He must have had an outlet, possibly a crooked market dealer or butcher. But I would go and see him anyway, and immediately.

'Just get them sheep back, Mr Rhea, never mind about a court. Ah'd hate to get my name in t'papers for summat like that.'

'All right,' I heard myself saying. 'If I get the sheep back, we'll punish him ourselves, eh? Alive that is – that's if we get your sheep back alive.'

'Aye, that's a deal. And if he's killed 'em and you can prove it, then take him to Eltering Magistrates'. Now that's what Ah calls a fair deal.'

'Or if I can prove he's stolen them and got rid of them?'

'Aye, all right. But if you get 'em back alive and well, we forget yon court?'

And so the peculiar deal was struck. I knew I'd stand little chance with Claude Jeremiah; he was cute enough not to keep the animals any longer than necessary, and I knew I would have a very slender chance of proving him to be the thief. But I knew it was him – in my bones, I knew.

My priority now was to race back to Elsinby and unearth him. I had to catch him before he disposed of the animals, and because he'd stolen them during the night, they could be seventy or eighty miles away by now, or more. I told Ted I'd be in touch if there was any development, and rode off in a cloud of spray from the damp road.

Thirty-five minutes later, I was cruising down the main street of Elsinby, and turned off the tarmac highway on to the rough track which led down to Claude Jeremiah's untidy collection of buildings. As I bumped along his road, I heard his lurcher begin to bark. Alfred, the dog, had warned him of my approach, and that's how Alfred earned his meat.

I parked the motorcycle and leaned it against a tree about fifty yards from the house and walked the rest of the journey. I saw no sign of Claude Jeremiah or of his pick-up, and so I knocked on the door.

Seconds later, the man himself answered.

'Oh, Mr Rhea, this is an early visit. Something wrong?'

'Were you out last night or early this morning, Claude?' I did not waste time with useless preliminaries. He knew the score as well as I.

'Out? Me? Good heavens no, Mr Rhea. I had an early night and have just nicely got out of bed.'

'You weren't out anywhere near Ted Williamson's place then? At Keld House?'

'Keld House, Mr Rhea? Why should I go to Keld House?'

'Looking for work, maybe?' I smiled.

'Ah, yes. I'd forgotten. Yes, of course. I did go to see him. I was looking for casual work, Mr Rhea, harvesting, potato picking, hedging and ditching, anything, but that was a day or two ago.'

'And he didn't have a job for you?'

'No, Mr Rhea, he didn't. Why, has he one now? Is

that it? You've been up there checking your livestock registers and he's changed his mind? He liked me and wants me to work for him?' There was a wicked gleam in his bright eyes.

'No, he has no job. But he has lost some sheep, Claude.'

'Sheep? Lost? I've not seen sheep up there, Mr Rhea, not me. Oh no.'

'Stolen, Claude. His sheep were stolen, and I know you were there.'

'Stolen? Not when I was there, Mr Rhea, surely?'

'No, last night, during the night or maybe early this morning. Eight gimmers, Claude Jeremiah, in a pick-up just like yours.'

'There's lots of those little Morrises about, Mr Rhea, lots of them.'

'So you didn't steal his sheep, then?'

'Now you know me, Mr Rhea. I'd never steal sheep, not me. I know I'm light-fingered and a worry to you, but I'm not a sheep-stealer. Not me.'

'Then you won't mind if I take a look around your place?'

'Mind? You've no right to search my place, Mr Rhea, no right ...'

'But you don't object, surely, do you? I mean, shall I radio my control and get a search warrant issued? Then our C.I.D. can come here, in force, lots of them, and really search your house and premises ...'

'There's nothing here, Mr Rhea, nothing.'

'Then let me see your pick-up.'

'It's in that shed.' He pointed to a shed with a large wooden hasp as its lock. 'There are some sheep there, as well, Mr Rhea. Don't let them out, they're waiting to be collected.' And his voice trailed away.

187

'Eight?' I asked.

'How did you know that?' he regarded me with a steady stare.

'With blue marks on their left flanks?'

'Yes,' he said, wilting now. 'That's very astute of you, Mr Rhea. I got them for a friend …'

'You stole them from Ted Williamson,' and I then remembered my unusual bargain with Ted. 'Show me, Claude, and no mucking about.'

Resigned to his fate, he took me to the shed and inside was his little vehicle, but it was jacked up and the rear tyre was missing.

'I just got home,' he said grimly, 'and was coming down my lane, when I got a puncture. There was a bleb on the inside of the tyre, Mr Rhea, so I got landed with those sheep … look, I'm sorry …'

And in a wire pen at the far end of the shed were eight gimmers contentedly chewing hay, their blue rumps readily visible.

'My spare had a puncture as well,' he said. 'It's not my day, Mr Rhea.'

'It is your lucky day, Claude Jeremiah,' I said. 'If you get those sheep back to Ted's this morning, he will not take you to court.'

His eyes lit up. 'Really? Mr Rhea? That's gen, is it?'

'It is,' I said, somewhat sadly, and then a car entered the yard. I looked out and saw it was the mechanic from Elsinby Garage. He climbed out and took a pair of wheels from his boot and trundled them over to this shed.

'Oh, hello, Mr Rhea. Not a bad morning. Claude – your tyres – one new tyre fitted and one puncture mended. Two pounds three and six please.'

'I haven't any money,' said Claude.

'Then I take the wheels back and you'll get 'em when you pay ...'

'Just a minute, Graham.' He changed his mind and dug deep into his pocket. He found the necessary cash and paid the mechanic who drove away contented.

'Now, Claude Jeremiah,' I said. 'Right now you replace that wheel and you take those sheep back to Keld Head. I'll wait until you do and I'll follow you to the farm. Right now, with no more messing about.'

'But, Mr Rhea ...'

'It's that, or court, Claude Jeremiah, and for sheep-stealing hereabouts, you're risking prison, you know.'

Without a word, he bent to the task of replacing the wheel and within five minutes, the truck was roadworthy. The spare was thrown into the rear, and I instructed him to herd the sheep aboard. He succeeded without a great deal of trouble, as they were already confined in the building, and within fifteen minutes, we were heading for Keld House.

Ted was delighted. His wife was overcome because some of these had been pet lambs, and I smiled as they were replaced in their paddock in exactly the same way he'd removed them. He reversed his truck into the gate, lowered the tailboard and shooed out the animals.

'Is that it, Mr Rhea?' Claude asked me, anxious to be off.

'Not quite, Claude,' I smiled at him, and I saw the look of anxiety on his face. 'You've a debt to pay, haven't you?'

'Debt? Here? I don't owe money, Mr Rhea, not here.'

'No, but if it wasn't for Mr and Mrs Williamson's generosity, you'd be under arrest and sitting in a cell at Ashfordly Police Station. You'd be waiting for a court appearance on a serious criminal charge and even prison.'

He said nothing, but lowered his head.

'Ted,' I addressed the farmer. 'This morning you told me you needed some hedging and ditching doing, and couldn't afford to pay anybody?'

'Aye, things are a bit tight,' he confirmed.

'Claude is good at things like that, he's very handy about a farm, Ted, and can turn his hand to anything. He won't need paying, of course, and he has volunteered to help you as an act of contrition.'

'I have?' asked Claude.

'You have, just now. You will work here until Ted has got caught up with his outstanding jobs. For nowt, Claude. You work for nowt, and if you go away, or pinch anything from here, or anywhere else, we'll activate the sheep-stealing charge. That'll get you several years in clink, my lad.'

'I'll put the kettle on,' said Mrs Williamson.

As we discussed the tasks that awaited him, I could see Claude wilting at the thought. We entered the kitchen for a celebratory cup of tea laced with a fair helping of whisky, and I recalled the old days of threshing and harvesting on these moors.

Everybody helped one another; they loaned equipment and manpower so that all could reap their harvests as quickly as possible, and I smiled to myself.

As I drank my tea, I reminded Ted and Claude of this system, which continued to operate in some areas.

'Can you remember the days when you all helped each other, Ted?' I asked, hoping he would recognise the drift of my conversation.

'By gum, aye,' he smiled. 'Grand days, them. Did thoo know, Claude, we needed fourteen fellers to work

190

on a threshing day. There was t'engine driver, forkers, corn carriers, stack builders, a lad to see t'engine allus had water, and a few more besides. We all helped out, thoo sees, lending men and machinery, moving across these hills and getting all these crops in as fast as we could.'

'You can still lend a man, Ted,' I smiled. 'I know Claude will let himself be lent out, for nothing of course. Didn't you say you were going over to High Rigg next week?'

Ted was quick-thinking and agreed with my fictitious work idea. I knew he would offer Claude to High Rigg Farm, and I knew the little man was fixed up for work for several weeks to come. All for no pay.

It would have been cheaper to have paid a fine in court.

And, of course, it would have been better not to have stolen those sheep.

But I still had not managed to win a conviction against Claude. I could wait. One day, he'd come. One day …

Chapter 9

'I have been in love, and in debt, and in drink,
this many and many a year.'

ALEXANDER BROME (1620–1666)

SERGEANT CHARLIE BAIRSTOW AND I were sitting in his
official car, discussing a spate of vandalism which had
broken out in the village of Elsinby. Our talk was not so
much a plan of action, but more a small symposium of
ideas for the total eradication of vandalism by
saturating the village with police officers. That, in
reality, meant regular visits from me. The time was
approaching ten o'clock one Wednesday evening in
early May and the night was dark, albeit with a hint of
brightness over the distant horizon.

We were not in Elsinby at this time; in fact, I was
performing a late motorcycle patrol across the whole
range of Ryedale and Sergeant Bairstow had found me
just outside Malton, on the minor road to Calletby.

'Evening, Nick,' he'd greeted me in his usual affable
way. 'Take your helmet off and sit with me a few
minutes.'

And that is how I came to be sitting at his side in the
tiny police car some distance off my own beat. We did
not make any great progress in our battle against
vandals but I enjoyed the opportunity to air my views
about this creeping menace, and the discussion added

welcome interest to my lonely patrol.

But as we sat and talked, I heard someone running towards the car. The darkness made it difficult to identify the sex or state of the runner, but soon there was a frantic tapping on Sergeant Bairstow's window.

'By, I'm glad I found you fellers.' A thick-set farm youth with corduroy trousers and an old tweed jacket was addressing us, having quickly opened Sergeant Bairstow's door.

'Summat wrong?' Bairstow used the local pronunciation.

'Aye, Sergeant,' the lad said. 'In yon barn of ours. There's a man and I reckon he's dead. He's laid out on our straw, and I wouldn't guess how long he's been there.'

'You've not touched anything?' asked Sergeant Bairstow.

'Not a thing, Sergeant, not a thing. Ah wouldn't touch yon feller for all t'gold in China.'

'Come on, show us then,' and Sergeant Bairstow opened the rear door. The youth climbed in smelling strongly of pigs and guided us to the barn. It was situated about four hundred yards along the village street, and down a narrow, unmade lane. The lad was called Alan Dudley and farmed for his father; he was on his way to a telephone kiosk when he spotted our conveniently parked car. He was highly excited and chattered about his discovery as he showed us the barn. There was no light, but he located a storm lantern which he'd left near the entrance, and produced matches to ignite the wick.

Sergeant Bairstow carried a powerful torch from the car and together we entered the dark recesses of the large Dutch barn. Alan Dudley guided us unerringly to the distant corners by clambering over loose bales and piles of unstacked straw.

He halted and revealed his find by holding his lantern high to flood the corpse with a dim light. Sure enough, there was the body of a man. He lay in a prone position with his head cradled in his arms and his legs curled up in what might be described as the foetal position. The fellow was dressed in a rough grey suit with black boots, and a flat cap lay on the straw a few inches from his head. His hair was filthy and had once been fair, but was now a curious shade of tarnished gold. I guessed he was in his late forties or early fifties and he appeared to be a tramp or a roadster of some kind.

'You came straight to us?' Sergeant Bairstow asked gently.

'Aye, I did,' said Alan. 'Fair turned me, it did, seeing that lying there.'

'You've not touched him then?'

'Not me, Sergeant, never. Not a thing like yon.'

'I can't say I blame you,' and as Alan stood aside, Sergeant Bairstow and I edged forward in the pool of light, treading carefully upon the straw. I watched as my superior squatted on his haunches at the side of the body and touched the whiskery face.

'Warm,' he said with some relief in his voice, 'and he's alive.'

'Alive?' cried Alan Dudley. 'He looks dead to me.'

'He's alive all right,' and Sergeant Bairstow lowered his head to listen for breathing, then swiftly sat upright, holding his nose. 'Drink,' he sighed. 'Meths. This fellow's a meths drinker, he's paralytic. God, he stinks!'

I went closer and sniffed the atmosphere. For my trouble, I caught a terrible whiff of the powerful odour which rose from this sleeping man. Alan came too, and creased his face in disbelief. The stench was terrible.

'We're fetching some sheep in here tonight,' said Alan, looking down at the visitor. 'He can't stay, some of them awd rams'll half kill him.'

'He's our problem, Nick,' said Bairstow softly.

'It's your car, Sergeant,' I reminded him, for my motorcycle was parked nearby.

'Help him into the bloody car then,' and with Alan lifting and sweating, and with me hoisting the limp fellow to his feet, we managed to half-carry, half-bundle the limp lump of meths-sodden humanity towards Sergeant Bairstow's car. With much puffing and panting, he squeezed him into the rear seat and laid him flat. The stench in the car was appalling, and I didn't regret being on the motorcycle tonight. I wondered what Sergeant Bairstow would do with the fellow, and realised with horror that I was the only constable on duty tonight in this section. The problem could be mine.

We thanked Alan for his help and praised him for his public-spirited action, but wondered what on earth we could do with the meths man.

'Follow me, Nick,' Bairstow ordered. I obeyed. I climbed aboard my Francis Barnett and followed the car for about two miles. Then he halted.

He left his car and approached me as I sat astride my motorcycle, awaiting further instructions.

'Nick, old son,' Sergeant Bairstow placed one hand on the handlebars of my machine. 'This character is yours for the night.'

'Mine?' I was horrified. I knew what was coming next.

'You are the only duty constable in the section

tonight, and if we take this character into the police station, he'll have to be placed in the cells because he's drunk and incapable. That means someone has to be present all the time, watching him and caring for him, making sure he doesn't snuff it or hurt himself. Someone has to feed and water him, fetch him his breakfast, and minister to his every need.'

'I'm supposed to finish at one o'clock,' I reminded him, wondering if I'd get paid overtime for this duty.

'Exactly, Nick. And I'm supposed to finish when I get home in a few minutes' time. So this fellow is a problem, isn't he?'

'Yes, Sergeant.' I wasn't quite sure what he was driving at, but was interested to find out. I knew the routine – a prisoner in the cells at Ashfordly Police Station meant all-night duty for the constable looking after him, and the tiny station was not really equipped for such visitors. There was no provision for food, for one thing. We could take him to Malton or one of the larger places, but I could imagine the wrath of the duty inspector if we presented him with our gift. No one wanted a smelly old meths drinker in custody if they could help it – there'd be the resultant mess in the cell to clean up.

'Well, Nick?' Sergeant Bairstow asked, after a long silence from me.

'Well what, Sergeant?'

'What shall we do with him? Any practical ideas?'

'Not really,' I had to admit.

'Well I have,' he beamed. 'Follow me.'

He started the engine of his little car and with the pungent fellow wafting evil fumes about the inside of the vehicle, Sergeant Bairstow turned around and drove towards Malton. I followed at a discreet distance and wondered what solution he had found. I was amazed to see him drive through the centre of the quiet town and across the river.

This was sacrilege! We were entering foreign territory now, because we had left our native North Riding of Yorkshire and were driving into the neighbouring East Riding, then a separate county. In those days, county boundaries were sacrosanct and jealously guarded. Although boundary rules were not quite so rigidly enforced as those in the U.S.A. during Wild West days, there was a great deal of professional jealousy between adjoining police forces. It was certainly discourteous to invade another Chief Constable's county without his knowledge and we all had instructions that whenever we crossed a boundary to make any enquiry, however minor, we must inform the local police of our presence. It was similar to getting one's passport stamped.

But this did not appear to concern Sergeant Bairstow. He trundled through Norton in our police car, and turned into the countryside with me close behind, ever vigilant for the appearance of an East Riding policeman. If one caught us, we were sunk …

The East Riding Constabulary differed from the North Riding Constabulary in those days, because the former wore helmets, whereas we sported flat caps. In truth, we had very little contact with these strange fellows from south of the River Derwent, and had no desire to meet them now. After two miles, Sergeant Bairstow pulled up outside a barn down a very lonely lane. I eased to a halt behind him and lifted the motorcycle on to its stand, then joined him at the car.

He spoke in whispers. 'Nick,' he hissed. 'There's an old hay barn here. We're in East Riding territory so be careful – we don't want them to find us. We'll put Meths Maurice in this barn, then belt back into the North Riding as fast as we can.'

'All right,' I said, for there was nothing else I could say. After ten minutes of heaving and cursing, we extricated Meths Maurice from the car and carried him into the cosy barn. I was dressed in motorcycle gear, complete with crash helmet, and Sergeant Bairstow was capless; had anyone seen us, it was doubtful if they'd recognise us as police officers as we undertook our nefarious deed, least of all the subject of our mission.

Within fifteen minutes we had our guest neatly laid out on a bed of clean new hay. He slumbered blissfully on and curled into his foetal position as we arranged the hay around him to keep him warm. Satisfied that he was slumbering peacefully, we left him to his new abode in the East Riding of Yorkshire. If anyone found him, he would no longer be our problem; his fate rested in the hands of the East Riding Constabulary.

Sergeant Bairstow congratulated himself on this piece of strategy and we returned to our own territory, hoping that no one had noticed our little convoy of trespassing police vehicles. I followed him home, but after twenty minutes, he pulled into the side of the road and signalled me to halt. I pulled up beside him and he lowered his window.

'Nick,' he said with a most apologetic tone in his voice. 'We've done wrong, you know. This is no way to treat our friends in the East Riding. Just imagine – they'll be lumbered with that smelly old character now, and besides, that barn might not be warm enough. If he dies, we're for it, and I'd never forgive myself.'

To cut a long story short, Sergeant Bairstow changed his mind and decided to return for the meths drinker.

For the second time that night, therefore, we crept into Norton and made our way towards the old barn. I parked close to the official car and together we entered the dark, cold premises. My torch picked out the slumbering form among the hay and Sergeant Bairstow said, 'Right, as before. Get him into the back seat, Nick.'

'We're not taking him to the cells, are we?' I was horrified at the thought of working all through the night just to look after this character.

'No,' he said, 'I know a nice warm shed next door to a bakery in Malton. We'll put him there for the night – somebody from Malton will find him and see to him. They've plenty of accommodation and staff. That will satisfy my conscience.'

What happened next was a most unexpected and unwelcome surprise. As we stooped to lift him from his cosy bed, the fellow suddenly hurtled from the hay and savagely attacked us. He beat us with his fists, cursed us, kicked us and began a most alarming and vicious assault upon us. He fought like a wild cat, cursing vilely and using his head in an effort to break our noses and cheek bones. He was not going to be taken anywhere.

He was shouting that he wanted to be left alone, and not taken to prison or hospital. We tried to make him understand it was for his own good, but Sergeant Bairstow's efforts to console him and reassure him were unheeded and there developed one almighty tussle in that barn. But two fit policemen are more than a match for a meths drinker in the long term, and in spite of his wild lunges, kicks and butts, we managed to quieten him and take him to our car.

I visualised problems persuading him to enter the

rear seat, but by now he was his previous calm self, and meekly allowed us to sit him in the back. Sergeant Bairstow was nursing a black eye and a cut lip, and I thought I'd dislodged a tooth, in addition to having a rising swelling on my shin from a well-aimed kick. But at least he was calm, and our enterprise could continue.

Thus we kidnapped him from his East Riding nest and conveyed him back across the river into the North Riding, where Sergeant Bairstow had another home in mind. We drove into the town centre and he located the bakery with its warm shed next door to the ovens. In the shed was an old armchair with horsehair sticking out and a hole in the cushion, but it was warm, cosy and dry. Once again, we manhandled Meths Maurice from the car and cajoled him into this new location. Fortunately, he was enjoying that happy state between consciousness and drunkenness and seemed to have forgotten all about the wild struggle of a few minutes earlier. He contentedly settled in the old armchair and his head flopped to one side, into the oblivion of a deep sleep.

'Doesn't he look happy?' smiled Sergeant Bairstow, wincing as his black eye bore testimony to his kidnapping.

'He's back home,' I said.

'He'll be fine; he'll sleep happily there until morning and he'll go on his way.'

And so we left him in his new place of abode. Sergeant Bairstow made his way back to Ashfordly, happy in the knowledge that his cells would not be polluted by this smelly fellow. I noticed he drove with the window open to rid the car of its pungent reminder of the man's presence, and his black eye would be a more permanent relic. I patrolled the section until one o'clock, but about twelve fifteen popped into the shed near the bakery before driving home. The man was still there, fast asleep in the cosy atmosphere, with his head lolling to one side in the battered old chair. But he was safe, dry, alive and no trouble to anyone.

I finished prompt at one o'clock that morning and at nine was back on duty in Ashfordly Police Station. Sergeant Bairstow came through from his house, and he sported a gorgeous black eye. I could not help laughing but he didn't seem to think it funny. He'd told his wife he'd done it as a ruffian knocked him over when rushing out of a pub, and asked me to confirm that tale, if necessary.

As I checked the Occurrence Book for the morning's messages, the telephone rang. Sergeant Bairstow answered it, and I heard him say 'Sir,' to someone.

'It's the Inspector,' he mouthed at me. 'From Malton Urgent. Don't leave yet, there might be a job for us.'

I waited as Sergeant Bairstow dealt with the call. There was a good many 'No, sirs,' and 'Yes, sirs,' and in the end, he replaced the receiver, smiling broadly in spite of his bruises.

'That was the Inspector,' he informed me. 'You know that old meths man? He went into Malton Police Station this morning about six o'clock to complain about the North Riding Police. He told the inspector he'd been asleep in a cold barn full of straw, when two nice East Riding officers, one with a helmet, had removed him to a warm barn full of hay. He remembers that but then, according to him, two awful North Riding Officers kidnapped him, assaulted him and made him sleep in a rickety armchair near a bakery. He's allergic to yeast and now he's come out in spots. The Inspector asked if we knew anything about it – he's checked with the East Riding lads and they don't know …'

'You told him 'no,' Sergeant?' I said.

'I said we had no knowledge of a meths drinker last night, Nick.'

'And he accepted that?' I put to him.

'He has no option – either he believes a drunken old meths drinker or he believes some of his most honourable officers. The man's fine, by the way, they've taken him to a place which will cure him, they hope.'

'You'd better keep out of the Inspector's way for a few days, then,' I suggested.

'Why?' he asked in all innocence.

'That black eye,' I said. 'It might take some explaining.'

My second problem with a body occurred soon afterwards, but the story really began during the First World War.

A farm girl called Liza Stockdale lived in an isolated homestead high in Lairsdale. She was born there at the turn of the century, 1900, and lived her first sixteen uneventful years on the farm. There she assisted around the place, looking after the hens and acting as milkmaid for her father with his busy dairy herd. Being always at work, she never travelled; she had never been to York and had not even been to Malton. Twice before her sixteenth birthday, she had visited Ashfordly on Market Day to buy livestock with her father, and that was the extent of her experience beyond the ranging drystone walls of Scar End Farm.

Then she met a soldier. A tall, dark and handsome soldier of nineteen chanced this way on an exercise, and he was in charge of a mighty gun which was being towed across the moors by a small platoon of young men. They camped near Scar End Farm, Lairsdale, and bought milk and eggs from Liza. As in all good love stories, Liza fell helplessly in love with this handsome visitor and to cut a long story short, she ran away with him.

They married soon after the 1914–18 war was over and lived in North London where her husband developed a successful business from a small draper's shop. They produced four lovely children who were a credit to the happy pair and in turn they produced a clutch of grandchildren who were also a credit to the family.

Back in the remoteness of the North Yorkshire Moors, Liza's relations continued to work on the hills, farming sheep and cattle and growing acres of corn for the cereal industry. Time went by, and the farming Stockdales prospered just as Liza had prospered in London, but there was one small blot on the happy horizon.

Liza had never returned home. Having run away, she felt she had incurred the wrath of her mother and father, and the scorn of her other strait-laced relations, consequently she never ventured back to the family homestead. Furthermore, she deliberately kept her address secret, and avoided all contact with her past.

Throughout her long and happy life, however, she'd nursed a secret desire to be invited to the moorland home of her family; her parents had died long ago but she had not attended their funeral at Lairsdale's isolated Methodist chapel. She had not been to the weddings of her brothers and sisters, nor to the christenings of their children. She had missed all this, and had often wondered about the Lairsdale branch of her family. Sometimes, she wished she had the guts to make contact.

Liza's husband, however, was not the insensitive man the family considered him to be. At the time of the elopement during the First World War, he'd been an aggressive, cocksure young man and it was his cavalier attitude and his worldly manner that had captivated the young Liza. On marrying him and settling down to a hard-working life, she realised she truly loved him and he truly loved her. Their love strengthened with the passing years, and Herbert often tried to persuade her to return to the farm, if only for a visit. He said she should write and make contact, but she never did.

Something intangible restrained her. Some unknown hand or force denied Liza the thrill of returning to her homestead, and she contented herself with life in London, the business and her family. Hers was a London family, not given to visiting remote farms in the north, consequently Liza's life bore no resemblance to her childhood surroundings and upbringing, and she had distanced herself from her roots.

Herbert never forgot that she missed Scar End Farm; he knew of her love for the area and made many attempts to persuade her to make the move. But she stubbornly and steadfastly refused. She lied when she said she had no wish to return; because she'd had to run away to marry him, her father had never owned her and the family had never made contact. She'd felt she was no part of that life in the moors.

Herbert's patience was infinite. He vowed that one day he would surprise her and take her home. She would not know where she was going until she arrived; he'd book a holiday in a nice hotel at Scarborough or York, and would hire a taxi to take her into the hills of Lairsdale and to the farm which he'd discovered was still in the family.

But somehow, that trip never materialised. Business was too demanding, the family too busy or time too short. Gradually, Herbert's intentions faded, if only a little, and that long journey from London to the heart of the North Yorkshire moors never took place. It was always something he'd do when he had the time.

And he never did have the time.

Finally, Liza died of a heart attack. One awful June day, a Mrs Liza Frankland collapsed and died in Regent Street, London. The post-mortem revealed she had suffered a massive coronary attack, and no one could have saved her.

Her caring husband, Herbert Frankland, a retired draper, loved her more in death, and as he wept alone that night he made a resolution that Liza would at last return to her native moorland dale.

He telephoned Pastor Smith at the Manse to ask whether she could be buried in his tiny churchyard at Lairsdale, and specified that it had been his wish to have Liza cremated. The burial, if permitted, would involve a small urn of Liza's ashes and Herbert alone would accompany them. All he asked was a simple chapel service to place Liza in her resting place, and he did not tell Pastor Smith of her family links with his district, save to say it was her wish to be buried there. He'd asked his own family not to attend; they'd paid their respects at the crematorium and this was to be his personal pilgrimage. He wanted to repay the wrong he'd done all those years ago.

Pastor Smith agreed without question and so the small interment was arranged for a day in late June.

Being a man without a car, Herbert Frankland left King's Cross Station in London in the early hours of that Saturday, carrying a suitcase and contents. In the suitcase were his overnight things and a dark suit for the funeral. Also in the case was a pleasant silver casket containing the ashes of Liza, his beloved wife. It bore her maiden name, Liza Stockdale, and was carefully wrapped in tissue paper, and tucked among his clothes.

The train left King's Cross on time and Herbert settled down to his long trip north, eagerly awaiting his arrival at York. A taxi was to take him across the hills into Lairsdale, where, at two o'clock precisely, Pastor Smith would conduct the burial ceremony. Liza would be home at last, resting eternally among her family and the moors.

At York, Herbert Frankland, sad and thoughtful due to the day's sorrowful occurrence, took his case from the rack, left the train and caught a taxi out of York.

At quarter past twelve, he was knocking on my door at Aidensfield Police House.

I answered the knock to find a lightly built man there, a man I'd never seen before. He was smartly dressed in a light grey suit and trilby, with a white shirt and a black tie, and would be in his sixties. He clutched a rather battered brown leather suitcase, and I noticed a taxi waiting outside my house.

'Yes?' I was enjoying a day off and was clad in old clothes, because I was in the middle of decorating a bedroom. I looked more like a painter and decorator than a policeman.

'Oh, er, is the policeman in?' he asked, smiling meekly.

'I'm the policeman,' I wiped my hands on my paint-stained trousers. 'PC Rhea.'

'Oh, well, er, I'm sorry to bother you,' he began, 'but it is important.'

'You'd better come in,' I invited him to enter my office. 'Will the taxi wait?'

'Yes, I've asked him to,' and he entered the small office, removing his hat as he did so.

'Now, sir,' I made a formal greeting. 'How can I help you?'

He placed his battered suitcase on my desk and opened it. Inside was a collection of assorted clothes and personal belongings, and I waited for some enlightenment.

'Officer,' he said. 'I left London this morning, from King's Cross, and I put my suitcase on the rack. It contained my overnight things, and a dark suit.'

I looked at the contents of this case. This belonged to a woman, for there were feminine underclothes, perfumes, slippers, blouses and so forth.

'So this isn't yours?' I guessed.

He shook his head and for the first time, I saw tears in his eyes.

'Would you like a cup of tea?' I offered by way of some consolation.

He nodded and I made him sit on my office chair. The poor man was obviously distressed, and at this stage I had no idea of the real reason.

I called to Mary and in spite of preparing lunch and coping with four tiny offspring, she produced two steaming cups. I closed the door and watched him sip the hot tea as he composed himself.

'I must have picked up the wrong case,' he said despondently. 'Mine is exactly like this one, Officer, and when I got off at York, I must have collected this. It's got stickers on, you see, and mine was plain, so I should have noticed, but I didn't spot them until I was almost here, in the taxi.'

'So yours is still on the train?' I ventured.

He nodded, and I noticed the returning moisture in his pale grey eyes.

'Look, Mister ...'

'Frankland,' he said. 'Herbert Frankland.'

'Look, Mr Frankland, there's no need to get upset. I'm sure we can trace your case very soon. I'll ring the British Transport Commission Police at York and ask them to search the train at its next stop. Let's see ...'

I made a rapid calculation, bearing in mind the time he dismounted at York and the time at present. I reckoned his train would have passed through Thirsk, Northallerton, Darlington and even Durham. With a bit of fast work, they might catch it at Newcastle, before it left for Edinburgh. During the time it remained at Newcastle, the railway police could search for Mr Frankland's missing case.

I explained to him my plan and he seemed relieved.

'Er,' he said after I had explained my intended action, 'There is one problem, Mr Rhea.'

'Yes?'

'In my case,' he faltered in his short speech, 'there is a small silver casket.'

'Yes?' I acknowledged, not having any idea of its contents.

'It, er, contains ashes, Officer. The ashes of my dear wife, Liza ...' and he could contain himself no longer. He burst into a flood of tears and I had no idea how to cope. I stood up and patted him on the shoulder, saying he shouldn't get upset and we'd surely trace the missing suitcase. After a short time, he dried his tears and apologised for his lapse, making a brave attempt to control himself.

I sympathised with him. 'I know how you feel ...'

I asked if he could give some indication of the location of the coach in which he travelled. Was it near the front? The middle? The rear? Before or after the restaurant car?

Gradually, I produced some idea of his whereabouts on that fateful train, and having satisfied myself on the time of his departure from King's Cross, I rang the Railway Police in York. They were marvellous; their well-tested routine would be put immediately into action, and when the train halted at its next stop, they would have it searched for the missing case. I described it and its contents, but felt there was no need to rub in the fact that it contained the ashes of Liza Frankland, *née* Stockdale. I then described the case now languishing in my office with its load of feminine apparel. Somewhere, a lady would find she had the wrong case, and I wondered if she would leave the train with Herbert's case and not realise the error until she arrived home. This could cause immense problems but I did not voice this concern to Mr Frankland.

'The casket,' I said once I was sure the Railway Police were in action. 'Is it recognisable for what it is?'

'It's a nice casket,' he said, shaping it in the air with his hands. 'The lid is firmly secured and on the side there is a panel with her name. It just says Liza Stockdale. I used her maiden name, because she's home, you see ... or she was coming home ...'

He told me all about his wife's links with this area, and I listened to his fascinating story.

'Is the casket a particular model? I mean, is it recognisable to someone like me?' I asked at length.

He nodded. He explained it was a standard make and gave the name of it; it was obtainable from most undertakers for cremations, and the name of the deceased engraved as part of the service. Mr Frankland explained her name was in capital letters, and it gave the date of her death, the sixth of June. His story helped to compose him and I felt it did him good to tell me all about his romance and marriage.

'Well,' I said eventually. 'The Transport Commission Police will search the train when it gets to Newcastle or Edinburgh. Are you staying in the area?'

'I'm at the Ashfordly Hotel, in Ashfordly,' he said. 'I've booked in for tonight. But you see, I had arranged for a funeral at Lairsdale at two o'clock today …'

'I'll ring Pastor Smith,' I said. 'If your suitcase turns up, they'll see that it is sent back to York and it could be back with you today; you might only have to delay matters a short while. Look, Mr Frankland, you go to your hotel now, and have lunch. Stay there until I ring you – I'll let you know the minute I hear something.'

'And Pastor Smith?'

'I know him personally,' I soothed him. 'I'll explain the problem and I know he won't mind. He'll be only too pleased to accommodate you at a time convenient to you both.'

I rang Pastor Smith and explained the situation upon which he readily agreed to wait. At this, the unhappy fellow seemed a little more hopeful and he left my office to resume his journey. I kept the case of women's clothing. I heard the taxi rumble away towards Ashfordly, and broke for lunch.

I did not know whether to laugh or cry over his dilemma. For the poor old man, it must be harrowing in the extreme, but the thought of someone's wife being lost in this way, was hilarious when viewed dispassionately. I hoped the British Transport Commission Police would locate the lost property before the lady passenger walked away with it.

I enjoyed my lunch, over which I explained to Mary the delicacy of this problem. Understandably, she sympathised with the old fellow and after lunch I enjoyed some coffee before resuming my decorating. Two o'clock came and went with no word from the Transport Commission Police.

At quarter to four, PC Hall from the Transport Commission Police called my office.

'Hall here, BTC Police,' he said. 'We've searched the entire train, but that case isn't there. It stopped at Thirsk, Northallerton, Darlington, Durham and Newcastle before we searched it, so the case must have been removed by the owner of the one you've got. She's bound to realise the mistake sooner or later and call us.'

'I'd appreciate a call, it's rather urgent,' I said.

'It's just a lost suitcase, isn't it?' he retorted, having dealt with thousands like this.

'No, it's more than that.' I decided to explain and he listened carefully.

'The poor old codger!' he cried. 'Oh, bloody hell! Look, I'll have our lads give the train another going over in Edinburgh, but I'm not too hopeful. I'll ask our Lost and Found Property people to check their records for today as well. The poor old devil …'

I rang Pastor Smith to explain the situation upon which he murmured his condolences, and then I rang the hotel to speak to Mr Frankland. I told him the result to date, but stressed the BTC Police were making further searches. He appeared resigned to the fact that his beloved Liza was lost for ever, but said he'd stay at the hotel for two or three days if necessary.

At five o'clock, I rang Ashfordly Police Station to

211

acquaint Sergeant Bairstow with the story, in case the BTC Police rang him tonight while Mary and I were at the pictures. He listened with interest and launched into a bout of laughter, telling me the old story of the woman whose husband had been cremated and who retained his ashes in the house. She had them put into an egg-timer, and her logic was that he'd never worked in his life, so he was going to damned well work now! Another had placed the casket of her father's ashes on the mantelshelf and someone thought it was pepper, while another accidentally sold her husband's ashes during the sale of the house contents after his death. His fate was never known. Sergeant Bairstow had a fund of stories about ashes of deceased folks, and I had unwittingly provided him with another. I failed to view it in his light-hearted manner.

Obligingly, he took details of the affair, with names and all the necessary facts, and said he'd cope if I was away from the house. I explained the need for Pastor Smith to know fairly quickly, and for Herbert Frankland to be told at the Ashfordly Hotel.

I went out to the pictures with Mary that night and returned home about eleven o'clock. The babysitter said there were no messages, so I turned in, tired but content.

Sunday was another rest day for me, and I intended to complete the painting and decorating which had been interrupted yesterday. Before doing so, I rang Ashfordly office, but got no reply. I wondered if Liza's ashes had been found, but felt I would have known. I knew the BTC Police at York would have called me, and I felt a tinge of genuine sorrow for poor Mr Frankland. He'd be sitting alone in the hotel, just waiting and able to do nothing.

At half past ten, I was in the middle of slapping some wallpaper on the bedroom wall, when there was a loud knocking on my front door. I cursed, but was obliged to answer. Mary had gone to Mass with the two elder children, for I'd attended early in order to get my decorating done. Grudgingly, I answered the door.

A large, unkempt farmer in his early forties stood there in corduroy trousers and a dark sweater, while a Land-Rover waited outside. I didn't know him.

'Morning. Is thoo t'bobby?' he looked me up and down, and I laughed an answer. I noticed he had a brown suitcase in his hand.

'Yes,' I said. 'I'm decorating. I'm PC Rhea.'

'Oh, well, this is important,' and he held up the case. Its significance did not register at that moment. 'Can Ah come in?'

'Aye,' I said, stepping back and he followed me into the office.

'This is a funny sooart of a gahin on,' he began in the broad dialect of the moors. 'Yon case isn't our lass's,' he said brusquely, 'but she got it off t'London train yesterday, by accident she reckons.'

'The London train?' now I was taking an interest. My heart missed a beat.

'Aye, she's at Univosity doon there and came up yisterday for a break. She's gitten a brown case just like this 'un, and somebody's switched 'em. Ah reckon somebody's got hers and they must know by now, so Ah thowt Ah'd tell you fellers. Well, there's neeabody in at Ashfordly, so Ah thowt Ah'd better come here, cos thoo's t'nearest bobby.'

'Did you look inside this case?' I asked.

'She did, and Ah did a quick peep. Nut a nosey peep, thoo knoaws, but eneeagh ti see it's a feller's suit

213

and bits and bobs. There's summat wrapped in tissue paper but Ah didn't oppen it up. That's nut my business.'

I lifted the other case from the floor and placed it on my desk, flipping open the lid. I saw the amazement on his face.

'Is this your daughter's stuff?' I asked.

'Noo that's a capper,' he said. 'Noo that's a real capper. Aye, Ah'd say it was her stuff, but she's in t'Land-Rover. Ah'll shout her.'

A tall, pretty teenager ran into my office, smiling at her father as he pointed to the case on my desk. 'Is yon case thine, lass?'

She blushed at the lingerie and clothing which was on display and said, 'Yes, it is. Good heavens … how… ?'

I decided not to mention the contents of the article wrapped in tissue paper, but did tell them about the poor gentleman who'd picked up the wrong case when he got off at York. The girl told me she'd got off the train at Thirsk, where her father had met her in the Land-Rover, and she'd not realised the mistake until late last night. She'd put her case on the top of her wardrobe at home, her toiletries being carried in a shoulder bag, and had gone to get the case this morning to do her washing. Then she'd found the man's stuff inside, and had not investigated further. This was the typical action of an honest dales person – they did not snoop into things that weren't their business.

I was highly relieved. I pushed aside the tissue covers of the casket and saw the silver beneath, but did not enlighten this couple of its significance. Now there were the usual formalities to complete. The girl would have to sign for her case in my found property register, and I would have to record her as the finder of the second case. Eventually, Mr Frankland would sign for his own goods.

'Right,' I said. 'You are the owner of the case of lady's clothes?'

The girl nodded.

'I have to make an official record of your receipt of this case,' I explained. 'What's your name?'

'Stockdale,' she said. 'Liza Stockdale.'

I had the name half-written in my book before I realised its significance.

I felt faint.

'Liza Stockdale? From Crag End Farm, Lairsdale?' I spoke faintly.

'Summat up?' asked her father.

'I, er,' I didn't know how to broach this one. 'Why is she called Liza?' I heard myself ask.

'Oh, it's after an aunt of mine,' he said. 'Ah never knew her, but she cleared off with a soldier way back in t'First World War, and never came back. My dad – that was her brother – thought the world of her and she never wrote or anything. He allus talked about her, my dad did. So Ah called my first lass after her ... just to keep t'name going, thoo sees, for my dad.'

'So the family wanted her to come back?'

'Aye, of course. Yon soldier was a nice chap, by all accounts, did the right thing by her, he did. We lost touch – she was t'only member of oor family to do a thing like that. Headstrong lass, they said, but all right, not a disgrace to us.'

'Is your father still alive?' I asked gently, my nervousness causing my voice to waver.

'Is thoo all right, Mr Rhea?' he asked me. 'Thoo's gone all pale and shaky. Aye, my dad's alive. He's turned seventy-five now, but he's as fit as a fiddle.'

'Look,' I said. 'You'd better sit down, both of you,' and I pulled up chairs for them.

'Nay, lad, thoo'd better sit doon!' he laughed, but he took the seat.

'I don't know how to tell you this …'

'Summat wrang?'

I did not know how to break this news to them. I could tell them about the old man waiting so patiently in Ashfordly, or I could show them the casket bearing this girl's name. Would the shock be too much for them, or should I tell Mr Frankland first? These were sturdy, practical folk, not given to whims and fainting sessions, so I decided to tell them the story.

'Mr Stockdale and Liza,' I said. 'Yesterday, a man called at this house with your suitcase. He'd come up from London and had got off at York, one stop before you, Liza. He mistakenly took your suitcase, and realised when he was on his way to Ashfordly by taxi. He called here and left it with me, and I tried to trace that other case, his case, which he'd left on the train. The railway police are still looking for it.'

She smiled, 'And I got off at Thirsk, taking it with me because it was the only one left and because it was just like my own …'

'Yes,' I said. 'Now, this is the sad bit. That old man was on his way to a funeral. His wife's funeral. She died last week in London, and he was bringing her ashes to be buried near her home.'

'Oh!' she said. 'And I had them in that case?'

I chewed my lips. She did not show horror, just sorrow for him. Her father regarded me steadily, and I knew I must now lift the casket from the case.

'Yes,' I said. 'This is the casket,' and I lifted the

216

tissue-wrapped casket from its resting place among the smart clothes of Mr Frankland. I removed the wrappings and revealed the name. I turned it towards them so they could read it.

'Liza Stockdale!' the girl gasped. 'My name?'

Her father's gaze never left me. 'Thoo means this is my Aunt Liza's ashes?'

I nodded.

'By ...' he said. 'By ... then she came home after all? Right back to Scar End! And by t'hand of her namesake ... noo that caps owt!'

I handed the casket over and his big, clumsy hands lovingly cradled it. 'Thoo said there was gahin ti be a funeral?'

'It should have been yesterday, Mr Stockdale, and Pastor Smith was going to conduct it. He wouldn't realise the Mr Frankland who arranged it was a relation of yours.'

'And that poor awd chap thowt we didn't care?'

'Yes.'

'Then thoo and me and oor Liza'll have to put him right, Mr Rhea. Come on, let's find him.'

'But I'm in my mess ...'

'That dissn't matter a damn, lad. Fetch yon cases – Liza, sign up, and let's be off.'

We found Mr Frankland sitting in the lounge of the Ashfordly Hotel, reading the Sunday papers. He looked pale and sickly, but smiled when he saw me. His smile turned to clear relief as he saw the young girl carrying two identical suitcases towards him. He stood up to welcome the curious party consisting of a policeman in decorating gear, a farmer and a pretty girl.

'You were on the train!' he smiled at Liza. 'I'm so sorry, it was all my fault. Is that my case, Officer?' The relief was evident in his voice.

'Yes,' I said. 'It's all there, intact, thanks to this young lady.'

Liza handed the case over to him.

'It's so kind of you,' he said. 'It did cause me a lot of distress.'

Liza was weeping openly now. She put her own case on the floor and said, 'Dad, tell him please …'

The poor old man looked horrified. I wondered if he thought she'd thrown away the ashes, or destroyed them.

'Nay, Ah can't. Ah'm all overcome,' and I saw tears of happiness and emotion in the big farmer's eyes.

Herbert Frankland looked at each of us for an explanation and I knew I had to speak.

'Mr Frankland,' I said. 'This girl's name is Liza Stockdale and she lives at Crag End Farm, Lairsdale.'

There was a long, long pause and suddenly, Mr Frankland flung his arms about the girl, crying 'Liza, Liza…'

On the day following, Monday, there was a large hurriedly arranged family funeral at the tiny chapel of Lairsdale, and Mr Frankland stayed at Crag End Farm for a long, long time.